"You're a virgin?" Luke interrupted, his expression one of total disbelief.

She made a palms-up gesture. "Well, yes. Why should that be so shocking?"

He stared at her. She'd never made love to a man, yet she clearly wanted to give herself to him. He felt wildly flattered, but more than that, he was shaken. Being a virgin at her age meant she was saving herself for marriage, or at the very least for the man she loved. The notion that she was setting her sights on him was a problem. One he had to deal with before they both did something they would regret.

"What you are isn't the problem," he said firmly. "It's what I'm going to do with you now that worries me."

She stared at him, her eyes wide, and then suddenly she smiled. "Oh," she breathed with blissful anticipation. "Are you going to make love to me?"

Dear Reader,

We've been trying to capture what Silhouette Romance means to our readers, our authors and ourselves. In canvassing some authors, I've heard wonderful words about the characteristics of a Silhouette Romance novel—innate tenderness, lively, thoughtful, fun, emotional, hopeful, satisfying, warm, sparkling, genuine and affirming.

It pleases me immensely that our writers are proud of their line and their readers! And I hope you're equally delighted with their offerings. Be sure to drop a line or visit our Web site and let us know what we're doing right—and any particular favorite topics you want to revisit.

This month we have another fantastic lineup filled with variety and strong writing. We have a new continuity—HAVING THE BOSS'S BABY! Judy Christenberry's *When the Lights Went Out...* starts off the series about a powerful executive's discovery that one woman in his office is pregnant with his child. But who could it be? Next month Elizabeth Harbison continues the series with *A Pregnant Proposal*.

Other stories for this month include Stella Bagwell's conclusion to our MAITLAND MATERNITY spin-off. Go find *The Missing Maitland*. Raye Morgan's popular office novels continue with *Working Overtime*. And popular Intimate Moments author Beverly Bird delights us with an amusing tale about *Ten Ways To Win Her Man*.

Two more emotional titles round out the month. With her writing partner, Debrah Morris wrote nearly fifteen titles for Silhouette Books as Pepper Adams. Now she's on her own with *A Girl, a Guy and a Lullaby*. And Martha Shields's dramatic stories always move me. Her *Born To Be a Dad* opens with an unusual, powerful twist and continues to a highly satisfying ending!

Enjoy these stories, and keep in touch.

Mary-Theresa Hussey

Mary-Theresa Hussey,
Senior Editor

Please address questions and book requests to:
Silhouette Reader Service
U.S.: 3010 Walden Ave., P.O. Box 1325, Buffalo, NY 14269
Canadian: P.O. Box 609, Fort Erie, Ont. L2A 5X3

The Missing Maitland

STELLA BAGWELL

SILHOUETTE *Romance*®

Published by Silhouette Books

America's Publisher of Contemporary Romance

Special thanks and acknowledgment are given to Stella Bagwell for her contribution to the MAITLAND MATERNITY: THE PRODIGAL CHILDREN series.

To Shirley,
A devoted fan

SILHOUETTE BOOKS

ISBN 0-373-19546-X

THE MISSING MAITLAND

Visit Silhouette at www.eHarlequin.com

Printed in U.S.A.

Books by Stella Bagwell

Silhouette Romance

Golden Glory #469
Moonlight Bandit #485
A Mist on the Mountain #510
Madeline's Song #543
The Outsider #560
The New Kid in Town #587
Cactus Rose #621
Hillbilly Heart #634
Teach Me #657
The White Night #674
No Horsing Around #699
That Southern Touch #723
Gentle as a Lamb #748
A Practical Man #789
Precious Pretender #812
Done to Perfection #836
Rodeo Rider #878
*Their First Thanksgiving #903
*The Best Christmas Ever #909
*New Year's Baby #915

Hero in Disguise #954
Corporate Cowgirl #991
Daniel's Daddy #1020
A Cowboy for Christmas #1052
Daddy Lessons #1085
Wanted: Wife #1140
†The Sheriff's Son #1218
†The Rancher's Bride #1224
†The Tycoon's Tots #1228
*†The Rancher's Blessed
    Event* #1296
*†The Ranger and the Widow
    Woman* #1314
†The Cowboy and the Debutante #1334
†Millionaire on Her Doorstep #1368
The Bridal Bargain #1414
Falling for Grace #1456
The Expectant Princess #1504
The Missing Maitland #1546

Silhouette Special Edition

Found: One Runaway Bride #1049
†Penny Parker's Pregnant! #1258

Silhouette Books

Fortunes of Texas
The Heiress and the Sheriff

Maitland Maternity
Just for Christmas

*Heartland Holidays
†Twins on the Doorstep

STELLA BAGWELL

sold her first book to Silhouette in 1985. More than forty novels later, she says she isn't completely content unless she's writing. Recently she and her husband of thirty years moved from the hills of Oklahoma to Seadrift, Texas. Stella says the water, the tropical climate and the seabirds make it a lovely place to let her imagination soar, and put the stories in her head down on paper.

She and her husband have one son, Jason, who lives and teaches high school math in nearby Port Lavaca.

THE MAITLANDS:

MEGAN MAITLAND:
Matriarch of the Maitland family. Her life had been filled with sorrow, excitement and joy. Once she was reunited with her long-lost son, she'd thought all would be well. But now strange things were happening at her clinic, and she wasn't sure who was behind the mystery. Was her dream of a maternity clinic going to fail?

JANELLE MAITLAND:
The oldest of black sheep Robert Maitland's children. Ambitious and grasping, she'd stolen and blackmailed and lied to gain the Maitland money. She'd been captured and sent to jail, but has broken out. Could she be behind the incidents? And was she representative of all the prodigal Maitlands?

RAFE MAITLAND:
The youngest of Robert's children. Hardworking rancher. He'd always lived life alone, but in the past few months he'd acquired a daughter—and a wife! Now he would do anything to protect his family....

LAURA MAITLAND:
Robert's third child. Vulnerable new mother. She'd swallowed her pride to ask for help with her child. She'd vowed never to depend on another man again, but Mick Hannon was very hard to resist....

LUKE MAITLAND:
Robert's second child. Luke was a loner with secrets in his past and his present. Although he was working as the gardener at the clinic, it was clear that his real occupation was much more dangerous. But even investigative reporter Blossom Woodward couldn't find out anything about his past. Or his future...

Chapter One

"**W**ho the hell are you, mister?"

The man behind the steering wheel shifted his gaze from the truck's rearview mirror to the woman in the passenger seat. He could say one thing for her, if she was feeling any fear, she was darn good at hiding it. Or maybe the young blonde sitting across from him didn't have enough sense to realize that only a few minutes ago on the grounds of the Maitland Maternity clinic, she'd come very close to losing her life.

"I'm a groundskeeper for the clinic," he answered automatically.

Which was true enough, he thought. For the past two weeks, he'd been working as a yardman for the clinic. He just hadn't bothered to let anyone know he'd been doing more than mowing grass and snipping shrubs.

Sarcasm twisted the woman's glossed lips. "I didn't realize Austin was getting so violent that groundskeepers had taken to carrying concealed weapons.''

He focused on the merging traffic in front of them before glancing once again in the rearview mirror. So far the gunmen were nowhere in sight. He believed he'd given them the slip about five blocks back, but in this evening rush hour traffic, he couldn't be sure. And he wasn't about to let down his guard. Especially now that he had someone else's life to consider rather than just his own.

''You better be glad I had a gun on me, lady. Otherwise you and I might be dead right now.''

Just as she shivered in her seat, he darted another glance her way. Blossom Woodward. She was the single reason, his only motivation, for coming to Austin. To track down the woman whose fresh face appeared every day on *Tattle Today TV*. She'd been sticking that pretty nose of hers into his past and now her digging had thrown both of them into mortal danger.

In his line of work, he'd learned many times over that people could never be judged by their outward appearance. Yet now, as he looked at her sitting only inches away, it was difficult, even disillusioning, for him to imagine that such a delicious-looking set of lips could spew such vicious gossip.

Across the seat from him, Blossom swallowed convulsively but still managed to keep her chin thrust resistantly upward. ''I'm not so sure those shots were fired at us. Or even if they were gunshots. You were so busy throwing me down to the ground, I doubt you know yourself!''

He jammed on the brakes to avoid crashing into the back of a double-parked delivery van, then, cursing under his breath, he gunned the truck into the left line of traffic. An insulted driver behind them leaned on his horn. Up ahead, the four-lane street was boggled with evening commuters. She got the impression that he expected those to part and allow them passage, like the Red Sea parting for Moses.

"Don't kid yourself, lady. Those were bullets flying around your pretty head, not exploding firecrackers."

The defiant toss of her head sent a long mane of honey-blond hair rippling against her back. He'd known she was a beautiful woman. He'd watched her on television and had spotted her several times going to and from the clinic. But this was the first time he'd seen her up close. Everything about her, from her creamy skin and blue eyes to her silky blond hair, sparkled and glowed with the beauty of youth.

"Just in case you hadn't noticed, mister, there were other people on the clinic grounds," she shot back at him. "Any one of them could have been the target. We might have found out what was going on if you hadn't thrown me in this truck and hightailed us out of there like scalded cats!"

He didn't bother to reply. The woman didn't have a clue as to what was going on and that was just the way he wanted to keep it. The less this sexy news reporter knew, the better off both of them would be.

A few yards in front of them, a traffic light glared a warning amber. He stomped on the gas pedal, sending the pickup truck flying through the busy intersection.

Gripping the edge of the seat, Blossom jerked her attention from him to the vehicles and pedestrians flashing beyond the passenger window. So far she'd not noticed where they were headed. She'd been too busy trying to gather her scattered senses together. But now she could see they were entering the outskirts of the city.

"Where are we going, anyway?" she demanded. "This isn't the route to the police department!"

"Forget the police, honey. They couldn't help us right now."

Her head whipped back to him. Wide-eyed and angry, she ordered, "Stop this truck! Stop it right now!"

Without bothering to look at her, he shook his head. "Sorry. I can't take that chance."

Blossom reached for the door handle, but her reaction was too late. He'd already pushed the electronic childproof locking system. She couldn't open the door unless he allowed her to!

"I'm going to file charges against you for this!" She pushed the words through gritted teeth. "This is—kidnapping!"

Grass stains marked her beige skirt. Oozy scrapes marred both her palms. Her shoulder ached from being slammed to the hard ground, and she'd lost an expensive tape recorder and shoulder bag to boot. If this man had been trying to save her life, she'd hate to think what sort of shape she'd be in if he'd been trying to harm her.

"Go ahead and file your charges. When the police hear I saved your life, they'll probably arrest me, anyway, for aiding and abetting a criminal."

"I'm not a criminal!"

Sarcasm turned up the corners of his mouth. "You might not be a criminal, Ms. Woodward, but your tongue surely is."

For a moment Blossom forgot that she'd just been

shot at and was now being carted away by a complete stranger with a gun.

"You know who I am?" Her voice was just as incredulous as the look on her face.

He grimaced. "Doesn't everybody in this part of Texas?"

She twisted around in the seat so that her knees were angled toward his and she was facing him head-on. "What does that mean?"

He hadn't meant to sound so insulting, but whether she knew it or not, this woman had already dealt him some misery. And no doubt her snooping had brought uninvited grief to other people's lives.

"It means if you can't find trouble to report on that so-called news show of yours, you stir it up yourself. Well this time, Ms. Woodward, you just might have gotten more than you bargained for."

His voice was too quiet, too smooth for Blossom's liking. Yet she told herself now wasn't the time to lose her nerve or her control. Even if those fired shots hadn't been meant for either of them, the man had saved her from getting hit by a stray bullet, she reminded herself. And so far, he'd not done one thing to harm her. But she didn't like being at the mercy of any man. Even a good one.

"Your thinking must be as twisted as a corkscrew if you think I had anything to do with that scene back there at the clinic! Do you honestly believe I, or anyone with *Tattle Today TV,* would stage such a thing?"

"I don't believe you really want me to answer that," he drawled.

Annoyance turned to simmering anger, but she did her best not to lash out at him. Her reporter's instinct told her she'd make far more progress with this man if she remained cool, calm and controlled.

"A few moments ago you were stressing to me how real those bullets were," she said pointedly. "Apparently you don't believe anything about the incident was staged. I think you're just trying to goad me."

He'd expected her to be determined, but not sharp. So that meant he'd already underestimated her. The idea grated on him. People were his profession. Knowing what was going on inside their heads was key to his survival. One thing was definitely obvious: he was going to have to stay on his toes with this woman.

"Maybe I was. Why don't you take the next few minutes and try to figure it out," he suggested.

Blossom had to bite her tongue to keep from flinging a retort at him. But she managed to remain quiet, and immediately her senses began to soak in the information around her like a dry sponge.

Somewhere in their flight from the clinic, he'd exited off the main thoroughfare and was now barreling at a high rate of speed down a service road that she'd never used before. The business district of town had rapidly disappeared behind them. Now only an occasional convenience store with gas pumps dotted the sides of the highway.

From what she could tell, they were traveling west toward the hot, hazy sun. Although it was November, most of Texas hadn't cooled from the long blistering summer. She'd worn short sleeves today and the air-conditioner blowing from the dashboard was none too cool on her bare arms.

As for the man behind the steering wheel, just the

sight of him was enough to raise a woman's temperature, Blossom thought. Generally, she was good about guessing a person's age, and this man looked as though he was closer to thirty than twenty-five. Crow-black hair waved loosely to the back of his collar. Equally black brows and lashes framed eyes that were a shade somewhere between dark blue and storm gray. Except for sideburns that grew to the midpoint of his ear, he was clean-shaven.

For some reason, the arrogant jut of his chin made her suspect that it had probably taken far many more whacks from a fist than it had kisses. But she could be wrong. He'd probably had more than his fair share of both. He was the sort of man a woman would look at twice, and that always garnered double trouble.

"Like what you see?"

His provocative question jerked Blossom out of her reverie and she realized she'd been staring at him for far too long. With a blush burning her face, she jerked her gaze deliberately toward the windshield.

"I was trying to figure out what sort of man you are," she said defensively.

No one could do that, he thought. Not even himself. He wasn't like other people. Other men. His life had never been close to normal. He didn't ever expect it to be.

"Don't bother," he said curtly. "You'd be wearing yourself out for nothing."

His odd retort drew her eyes back to his profile. "You're holding me hostage in this truck! It would be helpful to know whether you're some sort of gallant knight or a serial killer."

Spotting a parked car up ahead that was partially concealed on the side of the road, he eased off the accelerator. It wouldn't do for him to get caught by the Texas Highway Patrol. Too many questions would have to be answered and too many outside sources would learn of his whereabouts. He had to lie low. At least until he knew for sure whether those bullets had been for him or someone else on the Maitland grounds.

"I'm neither."

His brief answer infuriated her. She was a woman of words and she wanted to hear several from him. Mainly who he was and what he was doing carrying a gun.

"Are you…some sort of security officer?"

He didn't look at her. He didn't want anything on his face to give her any more suspicions than she already had. "What gave you that idea?"

She made an impatient noise somewhere between a snort and a groan. "It's no secret the Maitlands have been having problems. I wouldn't put it past them to have undercover security guards posted around the clinic."

"To keep nosy reporters out of their hair?"

She took a deep breath then let it out slowly. "Reporters are the least of the Maitlands' problems. But somehow I figure you already know that."

He'd not known anything about the Maitlands until he'd hit town a little more than two weeks ago. What he'd discovered had been very unexpected, to say the least.

"Yeah," he replied. "Maitland Maternity seems to be experiencing a rash of mishaps. But—I don't know anything about them. I just mow the lawn and water the shrubs."

For the first time since he'd sped away from the

clinic grounds, he settled his shoulders back against the seat and told his body to relax.

"I don't believe you."

Her retort didn't surprise him. Part of the woman's job was being skeptical, and he could already see that she was someone who viewed all angles of a situation. Not just the obvious. For that alone he had to admire her.

With a lazy shrug of one shoulder, he said, "Well, that's your prerogative. I'm just telling you that I didn't hire on with the Maitlands as a security officer. And you can do what you like with that information."

There were two things Blossom would like to do with his information. Prove it wrong, then throw it back at him. But that would have to wait. The first and most important thing she had to do was get away from the man.

"You still haven't told me your name," she reminded him.

"Does my name really matter? You don't know me. It couldn't mean anything to you."

"I have to call you something," she reasoned.

One corner of his perfectly chiseled lips lifted ever so slightly. "I'm sure you can think of plenty of things. Women have a knack for giving me labels."

Her nostrils flared as she drew in another long breath. "No doubt. But I think I'd rather stick to a birth name."

He didn't say anything for long moments, and although her eyes remained on him, she was acutely aware of the fact that they were getting farther and farther away from the city of Austin.

"You can call me Larkin," he said finally.

In spite of herself and the precarious situation she

was in, Blossom couldn't stop her gaze from traveling up and down the long length of him.

He was wearing a dark gray khaki uniform shirt with a pair of blue jeans and dark brown work boots. The Maitland Maternity logo, a simple oval with the initials MM, was sewn to a spot over his left breast. There was no name tag below it, and no name or job title was embroidered into the heavy material.

Yet none of those things were the real focus of Blossom's attention. It was the massive width of his shoulders, the corded muscles of his neck and arms, the leanness of his waist and the big brown hands on the steering wheel that all combined to mesmerize her. No one had to tell her he was a strong man. She'd felt his strength firsthand when he'd manhandled her into the truck.

"Is that all?" she prodded.

"That's all I'm telling you."

Her back teeth ground together at the idea that he thought he had the upper hand with her. Raking back a wave of hair that had slipped toward her right eye, she looked out the window and tried to catch sight of a highway sign.

"I get it," she muttered. "You imagine yourself as one of those stars who like to believe they're so grand they only need a single name."

If she'd been anyone else and the circumstances had been different he might have actually enjoyed sparring with her. But, as it was, he had too much on his mind, mainly what he was going to do with her now that they'd managed to escape the spray of bullets back at the clinic.

From the corner of his eye, he watched her cross her legs, then fold her arms against her breasts. He had to admit it was nice to see a woman in a skirt with silky stockings on her legs and high heels on her feet. He'd always been a sucker for high heels, and the pair on Blossom Woodward's dainty feet were the exact color as her classically tailored skirt and blouse.

She was petite and slender, but far from fragile. Her body was taut and curved in all the right places, and he wondered if she found time in her busy TV schedule to work out at a gym or if she was just naturally fit.

"Believe me, Ms. Woodward, there's nothing grand or starlike about me."

Maybe he wasn't a star. But he was far from ordinary. And how she'd ended up here with him like this was incredible. One minute she'd been on the sidewalk outside the clinic and the next moment loud pops were exploding all around her. Before she'd known what was happening he'd suddenly appeared beside her and whipped a pistol from a holster inside his shirt.

She wasn't sure how many rounds of bullets he'd fired at the vehicle skidding wildly through the parking lot. Thinking back on it, he'd probably emptied the whole magazine before he'd shoved her into the truck and yelled at her to stay down.

"In case you haven't noticed, we're out of the city," she told him. "No one is behind us. You can stop at the next gas station and let me out."

"I'll stop when we get to where we're going."

Panic sliced through Blossom, but she did her best not to let it take control. She had to keep her wits about her. She had to find out what this man was going to do with her and why. If his intention had simply been to take her out of harm's way at the clinic, his job should have been over thirty minutes ago.

"If you're thinking the television station will pay a ransom for me, forget it."

Before he could stop himself, he threw back his head and laughed.

"Now, who's thinking they're grand?" he asked between chuckles. "If I'd planned to kidnap someone for money, I would have picked a much bigger fish than you, Ms. Woodward. Any one of the Maitlands would be worth millions. What do you think you're worth?"

Blossom grimaced, mainly because he was making sense and she wasn't. Added to that, she couldn't think of one person who valued her life that much. She was a loner, a woman who cherished her independence. She didn't allow people to get very close to her.

"Not much," she answered. "*Tattle Today* has a cheap producer. And there are plenty of people standing in line to take my place."

Her answer was not what he'd been expecting. From what he'd learned about her and the show, she was a rising star and had already earned the nickname of Blossom the Barracuda. She was known for digging up people who preferred to remain anonymous and shoveling out stories that shocked and scandalized. Exploiting other people's problems was quickly making her famous.

"Your attempt at modesty is hardly convincing," he said with easy insolence. "There's not a line of people to take your place. Thankfully not everyone is capable of doing what you do."

Blossom was used to people insulting her work.

Mostly because her stories hit too close to home and no one liked to be reminded of their faults or weaknesses. Whether public or private, more often than not, she ignored the insults. She'd learned early on that she would have to have a tough hide to survive in her job and in life. Yet there was something about the barbed sarcasm in this man's voice that stung her more than usual. Maybe it was because she was already cross with him. Or maybe it was because she'd sensed, sometime during this crazy flight, that he was a keenly intelligent man and she wanted his respect. She wanted him to understand that she wasn't a barracuda. She was a woman who wanted to be the best at her job.

"Is that why I'm here in this truck with you? Because you don't like what I do and you plan to whip me into some sort of submission? Force me to denounce *Tattle Today TV?*"

He shook his head with wry disbelief. "My, my, you do have quite an imagination, Ms. Woodward."

Her hands balled into tight fists as she twisted around in the seat to face him once again. "You're being deliberately evasive! I want you to tell me what's going on! Now!"

He looked over at her, his black brows cocked with mocking inquisition. "Is that how you get your stories? You demand that people spill their guts to you?"

Realizing that her temper was getting the better of her, that *he* was getting the better of her, she forced her fingers to uncurl and her lungs to draw in a deep, calming breath.

"I've never encountered anyone I couldn't get information from,'' she said in a cloyingly sweet voice, then added, ''one way or the other.''

''Hmm. Then I guess this is a first for you.''

She glared at him. ''Why didn't you tell me to call you Mr. Wonderful? That would have been more honest than the name you gave me.''

He smiled, and even though the expression was meant to be sardonic, the flash of white teeth and an engaging set of dimples transformed his hard features. Like prey charmed by a snake, Blossom was momentarily transfixed by the sight of him.

''You know, you've called me everything from grand to kidnapper,'' he said. ''You're going to keep on until you actually have me believing I'm more than a groundskeeper.''

''You're insane! That much is becoming obvious,'' she said, pushing the words between gritted teeth.

He was half inclined to agree with her. He must have been insane to think the best thing to do would be to take her. But the whole event back at the clinic had occurred in a few short moments. He'd only had time to react to the danger, not to decide the best way to handle Ms. Blossom Woodward. Besides, he'd been waiting for a chance to confront this woman. He just hadn't expected it to happen this way.

''Look, lady—''

''You know my name,'' she snapped. ''Use it!''

Docile could never be used to describe this woman, he thought. Her blue eyes were spitting fire. Heat stained her cheeks crimson and her rounded breasts were heaving as if she'd just run a mile, or just made wild love to her mate.

The last notion turned his thoughts in a different direction, and for the first time since he'd learned that a Blossom Woodward existed, he wondered who the woman behind the blond beauty on the television screen really was.

"All right, Blossom. Why don't you settle down and have the good sense to thank your lucky stars I was around when those goons came by with their assault rifles."

Her brows arched skeptically. "Because I have no idea who you are. You might be one of them!"

He rolled his eyes. "Sure. That's why I shot back at them."

"That doesn't necessarily make you a hero," she countered. "You could have been in cahoots with the people in that van, but at the last minute decided to take the big slice of pie for yourself."

"Do you see me eating pie?" he asked as his gaze focused on the left-hand mirror outside his window. A vehicle was rapidly approaching their rear. The shape didn't resemble the gunmen's van, but in the past few minutes the sun had slid behind a hill and dusk was making it difficult to discern distant objects with much accuracy. He reminded himself how fatal it might be to let himself be distracted by Blossom Woodward.

"You know what I mean," she continued. "Those gunmen wanted someone on the Maitland grounds. And I don't think it was me," she said matter-of-factly.

He didn't answer until the vehicle had safely passed them and was traveling on down the highway. Even then his voice was preoccupied, something that she noticed and took as another insult.

"You're thinking too much, Blossom. You're wearing me and yourself out."

Frustration had her twisting around in the seat, away from him. The movement caused the heel of her shoe to come into contact with something on the floorboard. Looking down, she noticed it was caught on the strap of her leather shoulder bag.

Apparently she hadn't lost the bag back at the clinic parking lot as she'd first assumed. It must have slid off her arm and onto the floorboard when Larkin, or whoever he was, pushed her into the truck.

Thank goodness for small things, she thought. At least she'd have her identification with her if she was found dead or unconscious. On the other hand, if she was clever enough to escape, she'd have her checkbook and the small amount of cash she'd gotten from an ATM this morning. And last but not least, she'd have a comb and lipstick just in case she ever got back in front of a camera.

Forgetting her captor for the moment, she bent down and pulled the bag onto her lap. It was then she remembered the cellular phone inside. Why it had taken her so long to think of something so important, she didn't know, but her heart was suddenly pounding with excitement. If she could dial 911 without him knowing, she might possibly alert the operator that she needed help.

But where were they, she wondered frantically. If her sense of direction was still reliable, since leaving Austin they had continued to travel west and north. In fact, from what she could see of the passing landscape it appeared that they were headed toward Pedernales Falls.

The notion sent a chill slithering down her spine. The state park surrounding the falls contained more than five thousand acres of wilderness. Parts of it were rough mountain area. If he got her onto one of the primitive hiking trails or down in the gorge where the river had cut steep banks from the limestone, she might not have a chance to call for help. No one might ever see the two of them.

She darted a surreptitious glance his way. At the moment he appeared to be absorbed with the task of driving. If she could get the phone turned on and key the numbers without him seeing, then the dispatcher on the other end would hopefully pick up their conversation and sense trouble. Though she hadn't seen a highway sign yet, she believed they were on Highway 290. Surely she could repeat that much before he caught on to what she was doing.

Slowly, she pushed her hand beneath the leather flap on the bag. Her fingers immediately came in contact with more leather. Her checkbook. Inching deeper, she felt the bristles of a hairbrush, a wad of crumpled tissues, a tube of lipstick.

Triumph surged through her. There it was! Then just as quickly, she mouthed a silent curse. She'd been so happy to get rid of her old, heavier phone, for the lightweight flip-top version she was clutching inside the bag. But now she desperately wished she still had the old one. It would have been much easier to handle without drawing attention to her movements.

Oh, well, she couldn't be stopped by trivial hurdles now, she mentally scolded herself. She had to try. She couldn't let this maniac or whatever he was take her into a secluded wilderness.

Slowly, carefully, she used the tips of her fingers to tug the phone just to the edge of the flap covering the opening of the purse. Her heart was pounding and her mouth was so dry her tongue felt like a thick blob. Twice during her effort, she cast furtive glances at the man who'd called himself Larkin. Both times he was looking straight ahead, seemingly preoccupied with thoughts of his own.

Now was the moment, she silently coached herself. Flip the phone open and push the last digit on the third line, the first digit twice.

"What the hell are you doing?"

The unexpected sound of his gruff voice caused Blossom's whole body to jerk, sending the bag in her lap sliding to the floorboard. Immediately his eyes zeroed in on the phone in her hand and he mouthed a searing curse word.

"I'm calling the police," she shouted defiantly. "You're not going to take me anywhere!"

His hand lunged for the phone and ripped it from her grip.

Seeing the device as her last link to safety, Blossom cried out in horror, then, throwing herself at him, she began to pummel his arm and shoulder with her fists.

"Give me that phone—you crazy man!"

The truck swerved wildly from one side of the highway to the other as he tried to ward off her attack. In the back of her mind, Blossom realized she was probably going to make him wreck the vehicle, but at this point she didn't care. Dying in a car accident would be preferable to being murdered, tortured or both.

"Stop it, damn it! Before you kill us both!" he yelled.

"Give me the phone!"

With one hand he managed to shove her across the seat toward the passenger door. Before she could make another lunge at him, he jammed the brakes on and brought the truck to a jarring halt on the side of the road.

Without the restraint of the seat belt to hold her down, Blossom went flying toward the windshield and only managed to stop her head from whamming into the glass at the very last second.

By the time she'd collected herself, Larkin had rolled down the window and was about to make a fast ball out of the telephone.

"No! You can't!"

Shrieking now, she threw her whole body at him. But her efforts were too little, too late. The telephone went flying out into the hot night.

Yet even in defeat, Blossom continued to strike her fists against him. She wasn't going down without a fight. Not by a long shot.

It wasn't until he had her confined in the tight circle of his arms that he realized she wasn't just fighting him over a cellular phone. She was frightened and fighting for her life.

"Blossom! Stop it!" he ordered. "I'm not going to hurt you."

She went instantly still, her body stiff and rigid in his arms, her breasts heaving against his chest.

"Then—why don't you—let me go?" she asked as she gulped in deep breaths of air.

In the blink of an eye, his rigid features softened. "Because it's too dangerous. I—have to take care of you now."

Confusion crumpled her features and then her body sagged against his. The contact was as startling as it was comforting. Instantly, she was acutely aware of his dark face hovering over hers, the hard expanse of his chest against her breasts, the utterly male scent of his skin and hair enveloping her in an erotic fog. His hands were hot on the flesh of her back, yet she welcomed the heat, the sizzling excitement his touch was bringing her.

A fleeting recollection of something she'd read dashed through her mind. Something about fighting being closely akin to having sex. Well, at this very moment she believed the notion to be true. Her eyes were riveted to the curve of his lips while a strange need gripped her lower belly.

"I—don't—understand," she whispered.

"It isn't necessary for you to understand, Blossom. Just trust me."

With each spoken word, his lips drew closer until finally Blossom realized that as far as she was concerned, common sense, fear or trust were no longer issues. She had to kiss this man or die from the wanting.

Chapter Two

He didn't know how it had happened. One moment he'd been wrestling with her in an attempt to stop her flying fists. The next thing he knew her soft, warm lips were on his.

Ribbons of heat radiated through both his shoulders, and slowly it dawned on him that the source was her fingers pressing gently into his flesh. Yet those two spots of warmth couldn't begin to compare to the twin furnaces of her breasts thrust tightly against his chest. They were burning right through to his lungs, robbing him of his breath and his senses.

The small part of his brain that was still working told him that this was how a man slipped and forgot the dangers stalking him. It shouted that if he wanted to get killed he should just keep on letting Blossom Woodward dally with his senses.

The idea sent cold reality surging through him like an icy wave, and with it he found the strength to tear his mouth away from hers.

"What in hell is going on here?" He barked the question in a hoarse voice.

Blossom stared at him, her expression a mixture of dreamy bemusement and self-deprecation.

"What's the matter with you?" she snapped. Then, pushing out of his arms, she jumped back to her side of the seat and began to tug down the straight skirt that had ridden up along her thighs. "Haven't you ever had a woman kiss you before?"

"Not like that!"

Blossom's face flamed with embarrassed heat, but she still managed to meet his gaze directly. "I hope that's a compliment."

He groaned loudly, then said several curse words she couldn't have brought herself to say even if she'd been in a dark closet with no one around for three miles.

"It means you're crazy and so am I!" he yelled. "It means you could have just gotten us killed!"

Jerking his head to the right, he squinted through the back windshield of the truck at the darkness beyond. He could see no lights anywhere, but that was hardly enough to make him happy. Anyone wanting to slip up on them could have turned out their headlights and walked right up to the truck door, stuck a gun to their heads and blown them away without either of them knowing what happened.

Angry at himself more than her, he jerked the gearshift into low and gunned the vehicle back onto the highway.

Across from him, Blossom decided it was time she put on her seat belt. Escaping was not foremost in her thinking now. In fact, it wasn't in her thoughts at all. She was too preoccupied with her own rash behavior and with trying to understand what had prompted her to initiate the kiss that had just taken place between them.

Blossom silently groaned as the whole incident replayed in her mind. She had to admit she'd been giving Larkin more than just a kiss. She'd been making love to the man! As for him, she didn't know what had been going on in his mind. But hers was still generating X-rated images.

Had she totally lost her senses? she wondered helplessly. She had no idea who this man was or what he was up to. She did know that he was arrogant and insolent and he was holding her against her will.

Yet she couldn't stop the erotic thought that he'd also been holding her against his body as well, and she'd relished every second of the captivity. My word, she wasn't just losing her mind, she was turning into her mother!

Refusing to let that horrible notion remain in her head, she gave him a sidelong glance full of accusation and, God help her, appreciation.

"I fully intend to make you reimburse me for the cellular phone. You shouldn't have thrown it out the window!"

He flipped on the turn signal and directed the truck onto a dirt road. Dust boiled in their wake as he once again stomped on the accelerator.

"If I'd wanted to alert the police, I would have done so back in Austin," he explained with an exaggerated patience that grated on Blossom. "But you're smart enough to know that."

Darkness had completely fallen over the landscape, but in the arc of the headlights, she could see that the road they were traveling was carrying them deep into the woods, probably somewhere in the Pedernales park, she figured. She tried not to picture where they might be going or what tomorrow would bring. If she did, she would surely become hysterical, and that was a luxury she couldn't afford at the moment.

Peering at his profile, illuminated by the muted lights from the dash panel, Blossom asked, "Are you a cop?"

"No."

"A criminal?"

"No."

She took a deep breath and raked her disheveled hair back from her face with both hands. "A few moments ago, you implied that someone could or might be following us. Do you honestly think those goons with assault rifles wanted to kill you or me? Or both of us?"

His jaws tightened. "When you can feel the wind off a bullet, that pretty much implies it was meant for you."

Blossom wasn't convinced. "Look, I know I'm not the darling of Austin's reporters. I realize people frown on what I do and how I do it. But that doesn't mean they want to shoot me down. And as for you— well, to hear you tell it, you're just a simple gardener. I doubt anyone would risk spending the rest of his life in prison just for the kick of taking out a grounds-keeper."

"So you've got it all figured out. Guess you can put your speculations to rest now."

He was so smooth, so sarcastic, that she wanted to bash him over the head with something. Mainly her fist. But her knuckles were already sore from her earlier assault on him. Besides, she didn't want to risk ending up in his arms again. The temptation—or she should probably view it as the danger—was simply too great.

"I don't have anything put to rest," she retorted. "The last thing I remember before you grabbed me was that Megan Maitland, her friend Clyde Mitchum, and her grandson Chase had just walked out of the clinic. In case you don't know, Megan is more than just the CEO and co-founder of the Maitland Maternity clinic, she's incredibly wealthy and a very prominent and notable citizen of Austin. She dotes on her grandson, Chase. Which would place a high ransom on the kid's head. And let's not discount Clyde, either. From what I can gather, he and Megan knew each other in the past. He's come back to Austin to close the distance between them and so far Megan hasn't exactly pushed him away. In my opinion, those three are much more likely to draw attention from maniacs with guns than you and me. "

"You can't be sure of that."

Flustered and weary, she stared at him. "Can you be certain those three weren't the target?"

No, he thought with a silent curse. He couldn't be sure of anything right now. But as soon as he got Blossom and himself out of imminent danger, he was going to find out.

"I'm not certain of anything, Ms. Woodward."

Once again she crossed her legs and folded her arms against her breasts. The toe of her high heel swished up and down with agitation. "So we're back to Ms. Woodward now instead of Blossom. What's the matter? Afraid if you get too personal I'll try to kiss you again?"

He'd never encountered such impertinence or bravado from a woman. Especially one as young as Blossom Woodward. If the situation hadn't been so risky, he'd have the pleasure of taking her down a notch or two. But for now, he had to make sure she didn't get to him—in any way.

"You can try, but that's as far as you'll get."

Stung by his retort, Blossom clamped her mouth shut and stared out the passenger window.

She'd die before she touched the man again, she silently swore. He could choke her with his own hands or toss her back to those idiot gunmen. Either way, he would never be the recipient of her kisses again!

Nearly twenty minutes later, the pickup came to a halt in a small clearing. Blossom whipped off her seat belt and peered through the windshield. They were parked on a rough incline with the nose of the truck a great deal higher than the rear. In front of them was some sort of structure shrouded by huge shade trees.

"What is this place?" she asked. The words were the first she'd spoken since her silent vow to hate the man forever.

"A cabin that belongs to a friend of mine. Where we can stay. Hopefully, where we won't be used for target practice."

He opened the door and slid to the ground. When he came around and opened the passenger door, Blossom remained rooted to the seat.

"What's the matter?" he drawled. "Your legs won't work?"

Blossom wasn't sure if anything about her worked anymore. Especially the common sense she'd always prided herself in having. But the last impression she wanted this man to have of her was that she was a weak, helpless female.

"My legs are fine. But I'm not at all certain I want to go into that—house—with you," she told him frankly.

He shrugged, then lifted the baseball cap from his head and ran a hand over his thick hair. "Suit yourself. As for me, I'd rather eat and lie down on a regular bed than stay out here in the dark."

Not waiting for her reply, he turned and left her on the truck seat. Blossom watched his dark figure walk onto the shallow porch of the cabin, then disappear through a door. Moments later the dim glow of a light appeared in a single window on the front of the structure.

Apparently the man actually intended to spend the night here, she concluded. And since they were so far back in the boondocks that a bloodhound couldn't find them, he wasn't the least bit concerned about her taking flight.

Damn the man, if he hadn't thrown her cell phone away, she could have used it now. But that was mostly her own fault. She should have sat tight and waited for a better opportunity to attempt to dial 911. Instead, she'd panicked and tried to carry out the plan right in front of him. Stupid, Blossom. Real stupid!

With a weary sigh, she flopped over sideways on the seat and closed her eyes. She could sleep here in the truck seat if she had to, she thought. In a couple of hours, the night air would begin to cool. With the windows rolled down she wouldn't melt in her own sweat. But right behind that encouraging thought came the realization that the mosquitoes would make a feast of her. Just the thought had her rubbing her legs and arms in anticipation of the itchy pain.

Pushing herself upright, she gnawed fretfully at her bottom lip while staring at the cabin. Was there water and a bathroom inside? she wondered. Food and a place to lie down? If there was and he was enjoying those luxuries without her, she'd make him suffer.

Quickly, before she lost her nerve, she grabbed her purse and climbed out of the truck. Carefully choosing her steps over the rough ground, she stopped now and then to glance around her. There were no lights connected with other human inhabitants, no sounds except for a choir of frogs and katydids and the occasional call of a whippoorwill. She'd never been in such an isolated place in her life.

When Blossom finally gathered the nerve to open the door and step inside the cabin, Larkin was standing with his back to her at a crude counter made of wooden crates. He didn't bother to acknowledge her presence with words or even throw a glance her way, and Blossom realized that he'd been expecting her, as though he'd known what she would do long before she knew herself. The idea was unsettling. Even more so than being stranded here alone with the man.

"There's a bathroom on the back porch to the right," he said. "It's supplied with gravity-flow water. I'm sure you'll want to use it before we eat."

Relieved by this bit of good news, Blossom scurried across the room and out a narrow screen door. As he'd stated, there was a tiny bathroom built on one end of the porch, complete with sink, shower closet, towels, washcloths and bar soap with the tangy scent of pine.

After using the basic facilities, she washed her face

and hands, then brushed her hair and secured it into a ponytail with a rubber band she found in the bottom of her purse. Blossom didn't bother fishing out her compact. She didn't need a mirror to tell her she looked awful, but in this bizarre situation, comfort was more important than her appearance.

Back inside the cabin, she found Larkin scraping the contents of a large can into a black iron skillet. She watched as he placed it on a narrow cookstove with four gas burners, then touched a lighted match to the burner beneath the skillet.

"What is that?" she asked, inclining her head toward the heating food. "It looks like someone has already eaten it."

"Hash. It might not be gourmet food, but it will keep you from going hungry."

He stirred the blob with a wooden spoon, and as Blossom continued to watch him, she got the impression that he knew his way around a kitchen, even one as rustic as this.

The idea quickly spawned more questions in her mind, and she realized for the first time since the two of them had spun away from the clinic that she'd been so busy worrying about him having harmful intentions toward her that she hadn't stopped to consider his personal identity.

"You seem pretty good at handling that spoon. Do you know how to cook things from scratch instead of emptying a can?"

"When it's necessary."

"Is that often?"

He turned away from the stove and began to fill a graniteware coffeepot with water. "Whenever I want to eat something other than fast or frozen food."

"So—you don't have a wife who cooks for you."

"No wife. And even if I did have one, that doesn't necessarily mean she'd want to cook for me." He glanced at her as he spooned coffee grounds straight into the water. "Are you good in the kitchen?"

She had the naughty urge to tell him she was good anywhere. But she quickly bit back the words, shocked at her own brazen thoughts. Those bullets whizzing past her head must have done something to her. She wasn't behaving like herself tonight. Especially when she looked at Larkin.

"Not really. I manage to do canned soup or sandwiches."

His lips twisted into a mocking line. "Somehow it doesn't surprise me that you're not the domestic sort."

His barb shouldn't bother her. After all, she'd never cared about winning a Martha Stewart contest. She had other things on her mind, like getting the scoop on an adulterous city official before some other television station or newspaper caught wind of it. But for some ridiculous reason, Larkin's remark had left her feeling properly insulted.

"I didn't say I wasn't the domestic sort," she corrected him. "I just don't know much about cooking. There was never anyone around to teach me."

She was twenty-one, he knew that much. He'd also managed to garner other information about her. Such as the fact that she had no siblings. He'd learned she did have parents, but neither lived in Austin. Yet those were only outward facts about the woman. He knew nothing of who she was on the inside. Or why she'd been searching for a man called Luke Maitland.

"What about your mother?" He plopped the lid

down on the coffeepot, then turned and placed it on the burner alongside the heating hash. "Or did your family have a hired cook?"

In spite of herself, Blossom let out a caustic laugh. "Hardly. We weren't poor, but hired help of that sort was beyond our means. Although Mother would have loved it. She hated everything about domesticity."

He turned and, for the first time since she'd entered the cabin, allowed himself a leisurely look at her. She'd swept her long hair up into a ponytail on the crown of her head. The exposure of her dainty ears and long, lovely neck made her look absurdly young. Even vulnerable. An adjective he'd never expected to associate with Blossom Woodward.

"In other words, you didn't drag up a chair to the kitchen counter to stand in and watch while she baked cookies."

To his surprise she didn't come back at him with a flip retort. In fact, he was sure he saw a dark flash of regret in her eyes just before she glanced away from him.

"Not all little girls are lucky enough to have a mother like that," she said, then after a moment she slanted a pointed glance back at him. "What about you?"

Nothing registered on his face as he shifted back to the hash. Picking up the wooden spoon, he pushed it slowly through the warming food. "My mother is dead now. But…while she was around, she tried."

It hadn't been Veronica's fault that she'd had little more than roach traps to live in or barely enough money to put food on the table for four hungry kids, he thought. In her own way, she'd tried to make as much of a home as she could for them. Her untimely death and the brutal circumstances surrounding it had left a hole in him that he figured would never heal.

A few steps away, Blossom studied the distant, preoccupied expression on his face. At this moment he was far away from her, and she could only surmise that thoughts of his mother had tugged him to some other place in his past.

Larkin was a young man. Even if the woman had given birth to him in the latter part of her childbearing years and she'd died only recently, she couldn't have been old. The notion filled Blossom with curiosity. Yet she didn't ask him to elaborate about his mother. From his earlier comments, she'd gathered that he thought of her as a prying reporter. He wouldn't believe that her questions could ever be strictly from a human interest.

"My mother is in Florida now," she said as she made a quick survey of the cabin's interior. "With her fourth husband. She's been married to him for a year now. Much longer than I ever expected."

The small room contained a living, dining and cooking area. Along the front wall was a plaid couch, the green and orange colors faded and worn from years of use. To the right of the couch, in the far corner, was a small square table constructed of mismatched pine boards. Huge trunks of hardwood trees about a foot in diameter and twice that much in height passed for chairs. The area where she and Larkin stood was the cooking area, complete with a single iron sink covered with chipped and stained porcelain, a relic of a cookstove. Wooden crates covered with dusty white curtains served as cabinets.

Next to the table, across the back wall of the room, was a small doorway. Another dingy curtain partially covered the open space. From where she was standing, it was impossible to see what was beyond the curtain. She could only surmise that it was a bedroom.

"Are you saying your mother and marriage don't mix?" he asked.

She grimaced. "My mother likes men too much to stay married to one for very long. Her motto is too many men, not enough time."

He wrapped a dish towel around the skillet handle and picked it up from the burner. "This stuff is ready," he said. "Get some plates out of the cabinet while I carry it over to the table."

He hadn't asked her; he'd told her. But Blossom wasn't going to point that out to the man. She was hungry, and so far he'd done all the meal preparation. Besides, she was the type of person who could bend. Up to a certain point.

After a quick search of the cabinet shelves, Blossom found a stack of chipped and mismatched plates, cups and bowls. To one side of the dishes, stored in a plastic jug, was a handful of silverware. She dug out two forks and spoons and, after wiping everything off with a damp dishcloth, carried the dining equipment to the table.

Larkin dished the food equally onto their plates, and by the light of a coal oil lamp they began to eat the simple meal. Even if the globe had been washed of dust and soot, the primitive lighting would have still been dim. Across the table, she was barely able to discern the lines of his face.

"I've had candlelit dinners brighter than this," she said in an attempt to make light of their intimate predicament.

"I'm sure."

With each bite, she could feel herself growing more weary. Her shoulders and eyes were both beginning to droop, making her reach for the camp coffee he'd brewed.

"What does that mean?" she asked, while pouring the dark liquid into one of the cracked cups.

"Nothing. Just that I'm sure you've had lots of…dining out."

He made the word *dining* sound like a sexual romp, and she couldn't make up her mind whether to be insulted or flattered. Blossom realized she wasn't necessarily a raving beauty. Yet she was aware that the combination of her blue eyes, blond hair and lush curves were an attractive package to men. Even so, she'd never been overwhelmed with offers for dates.

It's that air of independence you have, Blossom. Men like to think they're needed and they don't feel that way with you.

Dena Woodward had often spoken those words of warning to Blossom. Even so, it wasn't in her to pretend to be something she wasn't. And anyway, she'd be crazy to take her mother's advice. Dena might know how to attract men, but keeping them around as a family member was another story altogether.

"In spite of what you're thinking, I'm not much of a socializer," Blossom told him. "For the most part men keep their distance and I keep mine."

Larkin shook his head with faint amusement. "You'd try to make a person believe water isn't wet."

She shoveled a forkful of hash into her mouth and chewed. After she washed it down with a swallow of coffee, she said, "I'm pretty sure I've never seen you before today. Yet you behave as if you know me better than your own grandmother. Have you been... stalking me?''

It was true that he'd come to Austin because of her, Larkin silently admitted. And it was also true that he'd been wanting to learn some things about her. Mainly why she was searching for Luke Maitland. But he'd certainly not been stalking her. For any reason. In fact, it was still hard for him to believe that fate had virtually dropped the woman into his lap.

''First of all, I never knew my grandmothers. Secondly, as I've tried to tell you before, Blossom, I'm not a deranged person. If I've been implying that I know you personally, it's only because I've seen you at work on television and made my own deductions about you.''

He could be telling the truth, but she couldn't be sure. For the past two months she'd had the eerie feeling that she was being followed and watched. The notion could have been all in her mind. But what if Larkin had been stalking her all this time, just waiting for a chance to abduct her. The idea sent a river of goose bumps over her heated flesh.

''Then that puts me at a disadvantage,'' she said, ''because I haven't been privy to any information about you.''

He shrugged as though she shouldn't view that as a problem. ''There's nothing interesting or necessary for you to know about me.''

''Are you from Texas?'' she asked. ''You don't sound like it.''

After he'd turned eighteen he'd never lived in one place long enough to acquire a local accent. His job had turned him into a tumbleweed that carried nothing but dirt behind it. For ten years he'd not had a family or home and he could only think of a handful of people he could call true friends.

"No. I'm not a Texan. Just a transplant."

The hash on her plate was gone so she put down her fork and looked at him through the meager light. Lines of fatigue were beginning to etch his face, but Blossom instinctively felt there was more to his weariness than just the stressful day they'd had. She couldn't imagine why the idea touched a soft spot inside her. Besides keeping her here against her will, he'd been nothing but a jerk.

"You don't want to tell me about yourself, do you?"

"No."

"Why?" she persisted.

Without glancing her way, he poured himself some of the coffee. "Because the less you know about me, the better."

She drew in a deep breath and let it out. Normally when she was interviewing someone it was very easy to keep her thoughts focused on the questions she needed to ask. But with Larkin, one look at him made her intentions fall to the wayside. No matter how hard she tried, Blossom couldn't forget how it had felt to be in his arms, to taste his lips. She'd never experienced such an electric state of euphoria and it frightened her to think how much she wanted to feel it again.

"When are you going to let me go? Take me back to Austin?" she dared to ask.

His brows lifted as he looked across the table at her. "That all depends."

"On what? Those people who shot at us?"

His smile had nothing to do with being amused.

"So you're finally accepting that we were the targets and not Megan Maitland."

"Not really." The cabin was hot and his close proximity was making it even hotter. She could feel sweat trickling down her temples and between her breasts. Her skirt and blouse would be ruined before the night was over. She hoped that was the only thing. "However, since you seem so adamant about us being the bull's-eye, I'm beginning to think you have enemies. I think that you recognized those men with the assault rifles and that you know why they came gunning for you."

His jaw like concrete, he rose from his seat and picked up their empty plates and silverware. As he carried the dirty dishes over to the sink, he said, "Like I told you before, Blossom, you're thinking too much. There's a bed in the next room. Go lie down and let me do the worrying."

Blossom didn't stop to consider her reaction. Like a shot, she was across the floor, clamping both hands around his arm. "Don't treat me like a child or an idiot! This is my life! And though you might play these sorts of games with other people, I don't!"

He glanced at her fingers digging into his flesh, before slowly and calmly lifting his gaze to her face. "Believe me, Blossom, this isn't a game."

"Then I demand to know what's going on. And why I'm a part of it!"

A blaze suddenly sparked in his eyes, warning Blossom he was on the edge of an explosion.

"You demand," he repeated with a snarl. "Look, little lady, if it wasn't for that big nose and even bigger mouth of yours, you wouldn't be in this predicament now. You've dished out a heap of misery to people and didn't blink an eye while doing it. Well, sister, if you haven't learned it by now, what goes around comes around. You're reaping your rewards!''

Fury hit her like the full force of a hurricane, and before she realized what she was doing, her hand reared back to slap him. But she never managed to fulfill the urge. Instantly, his fingers were gripping her wrist, forcing her hand back to her side.

''You won't be slapping me, Blossom. Not tonight. Or any other night. And furthermore, if you don't quit trying to hit me, you're going to get your backside tanned with the palm of my hand!''

''Why you...insolent beast! You have no right to do—''

Without warning his hands were on her shoulders, propelling her rapidly backward through the doorway with its dusty curtain and farther still until the back of her legs collided with the side of a bed.

''That's what you think, isn't it?'' he growled back at her. ''You think no one has a right to their privacy. If your digging and your questions expose someone to danger, you just mark it off as a part of the job. To hell with their life as long as you get your story. Isn't that the way you work, Ms. Woodward?''

Pain and humiliation burned through Blossom, and to her utter horror, tears began to sting her eyes. Damn it, she never cried. Crying was a sign of weakness. Besides, it didn't help anything. She wasn't about to let this man break her down to a sniveling female.

Furious with her own reaction to this man, she said, ''I'll bet you wouldn't be talking to me like this if I were male.''

He barked out a caustic laugh. ''You're right. I

wouldn't be talking at all. I'd have already knocked your lights out.''

And he wouldn't have had any trouble doing it, she thought with an inward shiver. The man was tough, strong, and he possessed a keen mind to boot. The combination of those three attributes made him a dangerous man. And yet she sensed he would never hurt her physically, or any woman, for that matter.

''I'll bet,'' she quipped.

His nostrils flared and then slowly his blue eyes began to glide over her face. One by one he inspected each feature, until finally his gaze settled on her lips. Hot lightning instantly arced between them. Blossom felt stunned, mesmerized by the desire to lean into him and feel the scorch of his touch.

Suddenly aware that the atmosphere between them had taken a drastic change, he removed his hands from her shoulders in the way a man might drop a snake, only after realizing he'd been bitten.

''In case you hadn't noticed, there's a bed behind you,'' he said sharply. ''Get in it and go to sleep.''

She opened her mouth, planning to tell him to quit ordering her around, but he didn't give her the chance to utter the words. Turning on his heel, he left her in the little darkened room as though he'd washed his hands of her for tonight. She wondered furiously how many more times the man intended to insult her.

''Aren't you going to tie me up?'' she called out to him. ''Or guard the door to make sure I don't slip off in the night?''

From somewhere in the other room, his low voice came back at her. ''We both know you're not going anywhere.''

"How can you be so sure?" she asked, each word coated with sweetness.

She heard the springs in the couch creak from his weight, and when he spoke again, his voice sounded as though he was bent over. "Because you have no idea in hell where you are or how to get out of this place. Added to that, you're too soft to try an escape on foot and I have the keys to the truck."

Turning slightly, she carefully felt over the top of the mattress. The way her luck was running there'd be a rat's nest or rattlesnake coiled up beneath the covers. But she couldn't worry about either. She had two choices: climb onto the bed or sleep on the floor.

"How do you know I can't hot-wire a vehicle?" she persisted.

She heard a thunk and realized he'd been unlacing and removing his boots. Apparently he planned on getting comfortable.

Unconsciously, her hand went to the buttons on her blouse. It would be heaven to undress, she thought. But to lie in here naked with him only a few steps away in the next room would be indecent and all too risky.

His voice suddenly interrupted her thoughts. "Because if you really did have that talent, you wouldn't have been stupid enough to mention it. And don't bother to get up in the night and start poking around for the keys," he added. "I have them on me. And I think you know better than to risk getting that close to me again."

Oh, yes, Blossom knew better. But at this very moment, getting close to the man was all she could think about. The physical attraction she felt for him was insane and certainly unexplainable. Yet she wanted to make love to him. Even more than she wanted to go home.

Chapter Three

When Blossom woke for the last time, sun was streaming into the tiny bedroom, the rich scent of boiled coffee filled the cabin, and the persistent call of a mourning dove drifted through the nearby window she'd shoved open sometime before morning.

Feeling as though she'd wrestled with a bear and lost, she rolled her head carefully to one side and squinted toward the door. To her surprise, the dingy white curtain was pulled completely shut over the opening. She'd not touched the curtain before she'd climbed into the bed or during her wakeful periods in the night. That could only mean Larkin had closed the curtain. To give her more privacy or himself, she wondered wryly.

Larkin. Her gut feeling had already convinced her that it wasn't his real name. And the man was no more a gardener than she was a heart surgeon. But just what was he? Who was he and how was she going to find out?

Don't be stupid, Blossom, she scolded herself. Finding out about Larkin was the last thing she needed to be thinking about. Escape. Now, that was the thing she needed to concentrate on. Not some arrogant man who considered it his privilege to take her as his captive!

You're not exactly a captive, a little voice inside her remarked. You're just not where you want to be right now.

Scooting to a sitting position on the side of the bed, Blossom glanced around her. There were no ropes or chains binding her arms or ankles. No locks on the doors or windows to bar her from going outside. If Larkin was holding her against her will, he was doing it loosely. Moreover, if he'd wanted to harm her or take advantage of her in any way, he could have done it last night. Instead, he'd given her the only bed in the place and kept his distance. The reassuring thought left her eager to face him and the day.

Standing on her feet, she tried to brush away the wrinkles in her clothes, but it took only a minute or two for Blossom to realize that the effort was useless. Linen was not the sort of material to look acceptable after you've slept in it.

Glancing helplessly around the small room, she noticed a tall chest of drawers crammed into one corner. If she had any sort of luck riding with her, she might find something in the chest to wear instead of a straight skirt and fitted blouse that both looked as though they'd been wadded in a ball, then crushed beneath the wheels of a dump truck.

In the top drawer, Blossom discovered several sets of sheets, most of them mismatched but still serviceable. She pulled out the second drawer and was rewarded with an odd assortment of old T-shirts. Plowing through them, she finally chose the smallest one of the bunch, a green camouflage garment with the word Buckmaster written across the front.

Blossom flapped the shirt in the air several times to remove its dusty scent, then tossed it on the bed before going on to the third and final drawer of the chest. Hoping to find jeans, she settled for a stack of hunting pants and was grateful to see that someone with a small build had once stayed in this place.

She gave the pants a good shaking, then, clutching both pieces of clothing under one arm, she stepped from the bedroom and into Larkin's domain.

Instantly, she realized he was nowhere in sight. An empty coffee cup was on the table, but other than that there was no sign that he'd slept on the couch or eaten anything for breakfast.

Fighting an unexplained sense of deflation, she tossed the clothes onto the couch, then stepped out to the front porch. With her hand shading her eyes from the rising sun, she peered out at his truck. The vehicle was still sitting where he'd parked it last night. At least he hadn't decided to leave her in this godforsaken place by herself, she thought with a great measure of relief.

"So you finally came to life."

The unexpected sound of his voice directly behind her made Blossom jump. She whirled around to see he was at the end of the porch, sitting in a straight-back, cane-bottom chair tilted on its hind legs.

He was whittling on a short piece of willow stick, and at first glance he appeared to be a man relaxed and at peace with the world. But Blossom wasn't fooled. There was an aura of electric energy surrounding him. He was ready and waiting for someone or something to happen.

"What are you doing?" she blurted out.

Slowly he shaved a curl of wood from the stick. "What does it look like?"

She padded closer, until she was standing only a step or two away from him. "Wasting time," she quipped, her eyes on the knife and stick in his hands.

The sound he made was closer to a snort than a laugh. "I thought that's what you'd been doing."

She was amazed at how good it was to look at him again, to hear his voice. "Sleep is essential to the human body. I don't believe whittling is."

"That's where you're wrong, Blossom. It's the simple things like carving a whistle that nurtures a man. Gives him time to think and allows him to accomplish something at the same time."

Her eyes drifted from the gentle wave in his black hair for a closer look at the piece of wood in his hand. "That's a whistle?" she asked skeptically.

"Just a minute and I'll show you," he told her.

She stepped closer and watched, fascinated by the deftness of his big hands. Carefully he notched the wood, then planed the end of the round stick to a gentle slant. When that task was finished, he put away the knife in the front pocket of his jeans, then blew the shavings from the newly formed whistle.

Her eyes widened as he handed the instrument to her. "Here," he said, "see if it works."

"But what do I do with it?"

His lips twisted to an oddly sensual smile. "Haven't you ever seen the Bogart movie where Bacall tells him how to whistle? You just put your lips together and blow."

Lips. Together. Of all he'd said, why did those two words have to stick in her mind like hot paste, reminding her of all she'd been trying to forget. But then he probably wasn't aware that everything about him sent carnal thoughts waltzing through her brain.

"If you're not going to test it, give it back."

His voice jerked her wandering thoughts back to the moment at hand and she cut him a querulous glance. "Just hold your horses. I'm going to try it."

Ignoring his watchful gaze, Blossom put the little stick between her lips and blew. The whistling sound that passed the hollowed space of wood surprised her. She hadn't expected any sort of sound to come out.

Impressed, she looked at Larkin once again and smiled. "This is neat. Where did you learn to make these?"

Her compliment sent warm pleasure surging through him, which in turn made him want to kick himself for being such an idiot. Most men would make monkeys out of themselves just to see a woman smile, but he'd never been one of them. And he couldn't let himself change at this stage of his life.

"An old man taught me," he answered, "when I was just a little kid."

Intrigued by him and the simple handiwork, Blossom turned the instrument back and forth in her hand for a closer examination. Then, unable to resist, she lifted it back to her mouth and blew again.

"I figure your dad probably showed you," she said after a moment. "Or did you have a dad?" she asked in afterthought.

Her question very nearly made him laugh. The idea of Robert Maitland doing something as mundane as whittling, especially for one of his children, was ludicrous. Between his bouts of gambling and drinking, he rarely acknowledged him or his brother and sisters. They were responsibilities he hadn't wanted.

"Barely."

She carefully watched his face. "What does that mean?"

Last night he'd been angry with this woman. Unjustly so, he realized. She hadn't forced him to come to Austin or take the chance of exposing himself. He'd done that all by himself.

"It means he was rarely around, and when he was, he wasn't worth having around."

"Oh, I see."

No, he thought, there was no way, even if she knew who he really was, that she could understand what his childhood had been like. It had been a relief when he'd finally turned eighteen and could legally strike out on his own. He only wished his mother had cut her ties completely from Robert Maitland. Maybe then she would still be alive.

"What about you?" he asked. "Do you have a father?"

She shrugged and looked off toward the distant woods. Tall sycamores and cottonwoods hinted that there must be a creek nearby.

"Sort of," she answered. "At least he and my mother were married when I was born. But that didn't last long. He's a blues musician. He plays bass guitar and travels with a band all over the place. I see him from time to time. But he's consumed by his music. Always has been. Always will be. I think in his own way he loves me. But he doesn't need me. You know what I mean?"

Instead of seeing Blossom the Barracuda, he was

suddenly looking at a young woman with tangled blond hair, rumpled clothes and bare feet. A woman who successfully hid the vulnerable side of her behind a tough facade.

"Yeah," he said, his thoughts making his voice husky. "I know what you mean."

Seemingly embarrassed that she'd said so much to him, she cast him an awkward glance. "I don't know what made me say all that. Now you'll be thinking I felt sorry for myself as a kid 'cause I didn't have a daddy on a regular basis. But it wasn't that way. Mother had too many other men hanging around the house for me to want one more."

She said the word *men* in the same way most people said *roaches*. Maybe that explained why she'd insisted she didn't date that much. Maybe her mother's parade of male friends had ruined her need for companionship of the opposite sex, he mused. But that didn't make sense, either. Not when that kiss she'd given him in the truck had been hotter than a firecracker. He was still trying to figure out what all that had been about. Just a ploy to divert his attention, then get away? No. She'd been clinging, he decided. Clinging as though she never wanted to let go.

"I don't think anyone would ever be guilty of accusing you of feeling sorry for yourself, Blossom."

A rueful grin lifted one corner of her lips. "I hope not. I've worked hard on my reputation. I wouldn't want anyone to think I'm anything less than a... barracuda. My job would be sunk."

He wanted to ask her why a beautiful young woman like herself would want to project such a tough image. Moreover, why would she want a job that prevented her from being the person she really was, at least for three-fourths of the time. But then, he could ask himself the same questions.

She stretched out her hand to offer the whistle back to him.

"You keep it," he told her. "That way if you run into any rattlesnakes around here you can blow it and I'll know what's wrong."

The word *snake* had her eyes darting around the porch and the ground surrounding the front of the cabin. Ordinarily the thought of poisonous reptiles never entered her mind. Her job rarely ever took her away from the asphalt and concrete of the city to the country, where snakes of a different sort roamed about. She was going to have to remember to keep her eyes open.

"Wouldn't a loud scream work just as well?"

He frowned as he looked away from her and out toward the rough dirt road leading up to the cabin. "You might have to use a scream for a different reason."

In spite of the early morning heat, a cool shiver slithered down her spine. Yesterday evening she'd not been ready to believe his theory about the shooting. The whole idea that someone might have meant to kill the two of them was just too incredible to accept. But now as she studied Larkin's serious profile, she had to rethink everything.

Obviously if he'd had intentions of harming her, he would have already done so. And she didn't believe he'd taken her for ransom. He didn't seem the sort that cared that much about money. She wasn't sure just what sort he was yet, but she was beginning to believe she could trust him.

"You still think those guys with the assault rifles might be looking for us?"

His gaze remained on the wooded area that stretched in front of the cabin. "I'm sure they're still looking."

"Why are you sure?"

"I just am."

The fact that he wouldn't elaborate only convinced her that he knew far more about the whole incident than he was letting on.

Trying a different approach, Blossom asked, "What are you going to do about it, then?"

Her question brought his gaze back to her face and she very nearly gasped at the hard resolution she saw in his blue eyes. This man wasn't out for answers, she thought. He was out for blood.

"I'm going back to Austin and do a little investigating of my own."

"When?"

"In a few minutes. But don't get your hopes up, I'm not taking you with me."

Her eyes widened at the implication. "You can't leave me here alone! What if they find this place and...and you're not here to...to get rid of them?"

The last thing he wanted to do was scare or worry her for any reason. It was just him and her together in this mess now and he needed her to be strong for both their sakes.

He made himself chuckle in order to ease the worried creases gathering between his eyes. "Last night if you'd been strong enough, you would have killed me with your bare hands. Now you want me to stay here and protect you. You must be a fickle woman, Blossom Woodward."

She shook her head at him. "No. What I really want is for you to take me back to Austin to my apartment."

His expression went grave. "I can't. Not yet."

She stepped closer and he was acutely aware that her knee was almost touching his thigh. The top button of her blouse was unbuttoned, revealing a shadowy softness between the tops of her breasts. He tried his best to ignore the provocative sight and the faint scent of her perfume drifting to his nostrils.

"Why?" she demanded.

"Because you would instantly call the police."

"What if I promised not to?"

He slanted her a rueful look. "I wouldn't believe you."

Her sigh was heavy with frustration. "So what would it hurt if I did call the police? If someone is trying to kill us, we need help."

"Not the kind they would try to provide," he said curtly.

She lifted her gaze to the roof of the porch and moaned with frustration. "Then you must have warrants on you. Or something."

"I'm not a criminal." But he'd been forced to hide like one, he thought. Forced to give up any sort of normal life for one that was filled with subterfuge and loneliness. And for what, he wondered wryly. To be a hero? To do the right thing?

She looked at him. "I don't understand any of this," she argued.

"It's best that you don't."

Her arms lifted then fell helplessly back to her sides. "What am I supposed to do while you're gone? Pray?"

He rose from the chair, and though he told himself to put at least a step between them, he didn't. Being this close to her was a pleasure he'd not felt in a long time.

"That would probably be more of a help than anything."

She tilted her head back to look up at him, and he noticed with a twinge of guilt that the rose color in her cheeks had vanished to leave her face milk white.

"What if something happens to you, Larkin? What if you can't make it back? No one knows where I am! I'll be up here—"

The shake of his head interrupted her rampant thoughts. "You can walk out," he said. "It would be a long trek, but not impossible."

If that was supposed to reassure her, it didn't, Blossom thought. Besides, for some crazy reason, she realized that she was far more worried about his safety than her own. Dear God, had he mentally manipulated her? Did she have that psychological thing that sometimes happens to victims and their captors? She must. She was beginning to believe he was the good guy!

"Why didn't you tell me that last night?" she asked, her voice rising with each word.

"Because it's not a trip anyone would want to make in the dark. Not even myself. Not without a light to see where I'm stepping."

She swallowed as the fear that she'd been brainwashed slipped away to be replaced by something far more dangerous. Larkin was so close to her that she could see the black bristles of his morning beard, the faint sheen of moisture on his bottom lip, the fine line of a white scar running from the edge of his forehead into his hairline. Heat from his body radiated toward her, sizzling her nipples and thighs and belly. She desperately wanted to lean closer, to taste his mouth, to fill herself with his hardness.

Blossom made herself breathe slowly in and out in an effort to get control of her reckless feelings. No man had ever had this sort of effect on her. She didn't know what to do about it.

"Now that you've told me I can walk out, does that mean you're going to tie me up tonight?"

Like searching fingers, his eyes slid ever so slowly over her face, touching each feature with lingering pleasure. "No."

"And what about today? This morning when you leave? I could walk out now that it's daylight. You just told me so."

"Yes. I just told you so," he murmured in agreement. "But you're not going to leave."

His certainty shook her. "How can you be so sure you can trust me? You haven't gotten some cockeyed idea that just because of that kiss I gave you I'll stick around and try for one more?"

A dimple came and then he was smiling, his white teeth flashing sensuously in his dark face. "No. Your life is led by your nose. You'll stick around just out of curiosity—maybe just to see if I make it back here alive."

He touched the mentioned spot on her face with the tip of his index finger, then turned and headed off the porch.

Stay where you are, Blossom, she silently ordered as she watched him walk toward his truck. You don't need to make a fool of yourself over this man. But the idea that she might never see him again pierced her like the thrust of a lance, and before she could stop herself, she raced off the porch and across the rough patch of ground between them.

Rocks and sand burrs jabbed her feet but she hardly felt the discomfort. Her only thought was to stop him.

Blossom caught up to him just as he was about to open the truck door. Her fingers latched tightly onto his forearm and urged him to turn toward her.

He looked down at her, the lift of his eyebrows conveying his surprise at her behavior. "What's wrong?"

Blossom's heart was pounding as though she'd been running from a pack of wild hounds. "Larkin, don't go," she pleaded. "This is crazy. Just stay here. After a while those guys—whoever they are—will get tired of hunting you and leave the city. We can go back and forget this ever happened."

She didn't know "those guys" were a small, ragtag faction that called themselves the Liberators. The radical group had been after him for months now, forcing him to go underground. The fanatical men wouldn't rest until they had killed him or gone down trying. But he couldn't explain any of this to Blossom now. She couldn't know until it was all over. And if he was dead then, it wouldn't matter.

"Blossom, don't get all sappy on me now. I've got to go. If for nothing else, to get food. You're hungry, aren't you?"

In spite of her need for food, her deepest hunger was for him, and she figured the evidence was all over her face. Which made her feel very foolish and him very awkward.

"Yes. But—"

"But nothing. I'll be back later. If—and this is a very big if—you do hear someone coming and you see that it isn't me, I want you to hide. Not here in the cabin. But in the woods—someplace where no one would be likely to look. Understand?''

She nodded as once again the faint thought that she'd become his devoted captive crossed her mind. "I'm not happy about any of this, Larkin."

Neither was he. Although he'd be lying if he said he hadn't been looking for this showdown. To put the violent faction behind bars where they belonged was the only way he could come out of the Witness Security Program and become Luke Maitland again.

"'Happy' isn't the issue here," he told her. "Safety is."

Blossom realized she had to relinquish her hold on his arm. But she didn't want to, and that feeling alone confused and frightened her. She'd only met this man a little more than twelve hours ago. That wasn't long enough to be feeling so possessive, to be wanting to throw her arms around him and hold on for dear life.

Frustrated with him and herself, she dropped her hand from his forearm and stepped back. "All right. I'll be watching," she promised.

Nodding, he opened the truck door and started to climb in, but at the last minute he paused to look back at her. She gripped the whistle he'd given her and waited.

"Goodbye, Blossom."

Something in his face and the way he said her name squeezed her heart. A silent sob caught in her throat as she stepped forward and into his arms.

The kiss he gave her was brief, but hot enough to rock the earth beneath her feet. Then suddenly he was in the truck, driving away, and she was watching him through a pool of foolish tears.

Chapter Four

By late afternoon Blossom was frantic. Shadows were beginning to lengthen outside the cabin. Hours had passed since Larkin had left her this morning. Darkness wasn't that far away, and the idea of spending the night without him was too awful to contemplate.

Larkin hadn't said how long he anticipated staying in Austin and she had been too muddled to have thought to ask him before he'd departed. In any case, she had not expected him to be gone for most of the day. A day Blossom had spent with all sorts of wild and dangerous imaginings whirling through her head.

With each passing hour, the frightening notions had grown to such mammoth proportions that all she could do was pace up and down the front porch and listen for the sound of his truck coming through the woods.

If she and Larkin had truly been the target of that gunfire, the assailants could possibly be hanging around his home or the clinic in anticipation of his return. The gunmen could be waiting for the opportunity to shoot him when he least expected it. For all she knew, he might already be dead.

The image of a sniper's bullet plowing into Larkin's chest nearly paralyzed Blossom with fear, and she could only wonder what had happened to her in the past twenty hours. She and Larkin had started out as strangers. Hostile strangers at that. Yet she'd already kissed him twice and had come close to it several more times. At this very moment she wanted nothing more in her life than to have him back here with her, to be able to see his face, touch him, and know that he was safe.

Blossom's tortured thoughts suddenly came to a halt as the far-off thrum of a motor caught her attention.

Standing stock-still, she peered toward the short distance of rough road and the deep woods that eventually swallowed it up. Was that the sound of Larkin's truck finally returning? she wondered. Or had the gunmen somehow managed to scent out their trail and follow it here to the cabin?

The last terrorizing thought sent her flying off the east end of the porch and racing toward the nearest stand of trees. By the time she positioned herself behind the trunk of a massive post oak, her chest was heaving and her heart was racing so fast she was light-headed.

As she gulped in short, painful breaths, her eyes darted from the cabin to the area around her hiding place. From this vantage point, she was fairly certain she couldn't be seen from the cabin. But if anyone decided to search beyond the house, she would be found immediately.

If you see that it isn't me, I want you to hide. Larkin's words of warning tossed from one side of her brain to the other while the hum of the motor was growing louder with each ragged breath she took. Her initial instinct was to run just as hard and fast as she could into the deeper part of the woods.

But the approaching vehicle could be Larkin returning, she tried to reason with herself. If that was the case, she had to hang close. Otherwise, he'd find her missing and be worried that she'd made an attempt to get back to Austin. Or even worse, that the gunmen had gotten her!

Oh, dear God, she prayed, please let it be Larkin.

With her heartbeat pounding a loud drumbeat in her ears, she eased her head around the tree trunk just far enough to glimpse the part of the road that emerged from the woods.

Blossom stood frozen, not daring to move a muscle as she waited for what seemed like an eon for the vehicle to make an appearance. When the nose of Larkin's truck finally came into view, she went so limp with relief that it was several moments before she could push herself away from the rough trunk and head back to the cabin.

"Larkin! Larkin!"

Halfway to the porch, he heard Blossom's voice. Stopping in his tracks, he directed his gaze toward the sound and immediately spotted her racing out of the woods, her blond hair and bare feet flying.

Once she reached him, she didn't stop or speak one word. She threw herself against him and wrapped her arms tightly around his waist.

For a moment he was so stunned that all he could do was simply stare down at the head buried against the middle of this chest. Then the trembling warmth of her body pervaded his shocked senses and his arms automatically wrapped around her, drawing her even closer to him.

"Blossom, you're quivering! What is it? What's happened?"

Her response was to shake her head against his chest and tighten her hold on him.

"Has anyone else been here since I left?" he demanded, as concern for her well-being overshadowed every other thought in his mind.

"No," she said, her voice muffled by the folds of his shirt. "No, I'm just—" She tilted her head back in order to look at his face. "I'm so glad you're back. And that you're safe!"

Her declaration, coupled with the tight grip she had around his ribs, took Luke by total surprise. He'd never had anyone make such a fuss over him. Not the colleagues he'd once worked with or any member of his broken family.

"Of course I'm okay," he said in a bewildered voice. "Don't tell me you've been worried."

She nodded jerkily, and he was further amazed to see her blink away a sheen of moisture glazing her eyes.

"All day long I've been visualizing you shot and bleeding. I kept imagining those gunmen had found you."

Luke knew he should pry her arms from around him and end the embrace. He should tease her and tell her that if he hadn't come back, her troubles would have been over. But he couldn't bring himself to do either.

For years now his job had been to protect people whose jobs or fame had thrust them into the public eye. If bullets were fired, it had been his duty to make sure he would be standing in the path to stop them. Luke had always considered himself as expendable. The safety of the client was the only thing that ever mattered to anyone.

To have Blossom behaving as though he was important to her turned a spot in the middle of Luke's chest as soft as gooey candy.

Feeling more than awkward, he said, "I was never in danger, Blossom. You shouldn't have fretted."

"You could have been in danger!" she exclaimed, then a smile broke across her face, and for further proof that he was actually back and all in one piece, she ran her hands over his chest, across the broad planes of his shoulders, then finally she cupped his face between her palms. "You don't know how hard I prayed that you would be safe today."

Never would he have connected Blossom Woodward with the act of praying, much less imagine that her prayers would be conducted for his sake. The idea implied that she cared. Luke tried not to believe it, but he could plainly see that the joy and relief on her face were very real.

"You're making too much of this," he said huskily, then before he got to liking all this feminine attention, he pulled her hands down from his face and stepped back out of reach.

She frowned at him. "Last night you scolded me for not taking the situation seriously enough," she reminded. "What's with you, anyway?"

There was a whole lot *with him,* he thought crossly. Mainly the fact that he didn't want Blossom to get all sappy over him. He had a job to do. All of his senses needed to be alert, but they wouldn't be if he had to deal with a clinging woman. Besides, he didn't want anyone to care about him. The few that had were now lost to him for one reason or another. He didn't want Blossom included in that group.

"I'm just trying to tell you that—" He couldn't go on as her blue eyes caressed his face like a lover's yearning hand. "Stop it, Blossom!"

The sudden sharpness in his voice caused her eyes to widen. "Stop what? What are you talking about?"

Either she was good at playing innocent, which he figured she'd practiced to perfection, or she really wasn't aware of what she was doing. Hoping it was the latter, he shook his head. "Stop looking at me like you—"

A knowing smile slowly lifted the corners of her lips. Luke was instantly reminded of this morning and the impulsive kiss they'd shared. Even though the contact had been brief, just the memory of it sent sizzles right through him.

"Like I want to kiss you—or something?" she asked softly.

He wasn't about to have her explain the "or something." Blossom was not a bashful woman. She would probably have no qualms about giving him a detailed definition.

Grimacing now, he turned and reached for a grocery bag resting on the truck seat. "I've brought a few food items back with me. Let's go inside and I'll put this stuff away."

The evening was still very warm. Blossom had

opened up all the windows in the little house in order to catch what breeze there was, yet the room was still sultry.

As Luke placed the groceries on the cabinet counter, he glanced from the fluttering curtains to her. "I guess this hasn't been the most comfortable place you've ever stayed in."

She shrugged. "No. But I've managed. The heat hasn't been bothering me." Only you, she wanted to add.

"I see you found some clothes to change into. You couldn't find any shoes to go with that outfit?"

Blossom glanced regretfully down at her bare feet. "No. High heels don't exactly go with hunting fashion."

He rolled his eyes. "Well, if you're going to traipse around outside, you'd better remember to put them on. Otherwise you're going to be bitten by fire ants or have sand burrs sticking in the soles of your feet."

"I've already encountered both," she told him. "But I'll live. I mean, what's a little ant bite compared to a trip through Austin rush hour with you."

Spunky. The word came to mind as he fought to keep a grin off his face. So far she'd proved to him that she was able to adapt. But for how long? he wondered. And what would she do once she discovered he was the man she'd been searching for?

Turning his back to her, he began to place the canned goods he'd purchased on the crude wooden shelf. After a moment he could feel her moving up behind him. Where she was concerned, his body seemed to have heat-seeking radar.

"What happened in Austin?" she asked. "Did you manage to find out anything?"

Pulling a newspaper from the brown paper sack, he turned and offered it to her. "I'll let you read for yourself," he said.

She eagerly snatched the paper from his hand and hurried over to the table. Taking a seat on one of the stumps, she opened to the front page.

Headlines blared out at her: Shooting at Maitland Maternity Clinic. Then in a smaller caption beneath: Austin Businesswoman Target of Gunfire.

Blossom glanced at Larkin. "Obviously the paper believes Megan Maitland was the target. Just like I told you. But I wonder what they think *we* were? Or maybe no one realized the two of us were around when the shooting took place?"

"Read on," he said without commenting.

With an impatient toss of her head, she focused her attention back on the daily city newspaper. Two separate articles had been written about the incident, both of them taking up most of the front page and a major portion of the second.

Much had been written about the Maitlands and the troubles the family had been experiencing both at home and at the clinic. Already aware of those facts, Blossom hurriedly scanned the article, her main objective to see if the gunmen had been arrested or at least identified. To her great disappointment, neither had happened.

"The police haven't caught them," she said grimly. "And from the way this reads, none of the witnesses were quick enough to get the license plate number of the van."

Easing down on the opposite stool from her, he said, "When gunfire sounds, most people aren't brave enough to stick around and try to jot down car license plate numbers."

Blossom glanced across the small table at him. His expression was flat, telling her nothing.

"They don't have much to go on, do they?" she asked.

One broad shoulder lifted and fell. "Shell casings and a vague description of the vehicle. If they have anything else, they're not divulging the information to the press. Which any smart police commissioner would know not to do."

Her lips twisted to a smirk. "You just don't like the press in any form, do you?"

"No. They always made my job even harder."

Propping her chin on her fist, she looked at him curiously. "Hmm. I can't see where the press would affect a gardener's work."

Damn it, he was slipping badly. And *she* was the reason. Her beauty and youth and vibrancy combined to make her a lethal combination for a man. When she was near, the atoms in his brain seemed to turn to mush. Oh, well, he thought, it wouldn't hurt to divulge a little bit about himself. Better that than to try to cover the slip and make her even more suspicious.

"I haven't always worked as a gardener," he admitted. "I used to be...in the security business."

She continued to study him with her blue eyes and Luke could see that she was waiting for him to go on.

"FBI? CIA?"

He chuckled. "Surely I don't have that look."

No, she thought, he resembled a member of a motorcycle gang more than a security agent. Yet in spite of his rough outer appearance, Blossom realized she'd never seen any man who looked better to her.

Shaken by the notion, she dropped her gaze from his face to the paper on the table. "Oh, I don't know," she said with slow thoughtfulness. "With a shave, haircut and conservative suit you might fit the part."

"With a look like that I could fit many parts," he reasoned. "Broker, lawyer, businessman—"

"No," she interrupted with a shake of her head. "Those occupations don't fit you. Whatever you used to do—well, I have a feeling you lived on the edge of danger. You wanted it that way because you liked it."

She was getting so close to the truth, he almost squirmed in his seat. But he didn't. Instead, he immediately tapped the open paper with his forefinger.

"I'm not news. This is."

Blossom's gaze followed the direction in which his tanned finger was pointing. Aloud, she read, "Local TV Celebrity Missing." She looked up at him. "But what about you?"

His lips twisted mockingly. "I'm not a celebrity. Just a groundskeeper. I don't count."

Ignoring his sarcasm, she turned her attention back to the newspaper, which went on to mention that she and a groundskeeper for the clinic had both turned up missing after the shooting yesterday evening. So far the authorities had no clue as to what, if any, connection their disappearance had to the whole incident. However, one eyewitness had stated that moments after the gunfire he'd seen Blossom and a man with a gun leave the clinic grounds together.

Then, shocked by the next sentence, she reread it

aloud, "The television station is offering a substantial reward for any information that might lead to Ms. Woodward's safe return."

She looked at Larkin in disbelief. "I can't believe they want me back *that* much. The producer is always telling me I can easily be replaced."

"That doesn't mean they want you killed. Besides, you ought to have known that's a bluff to keep you under his thumb."

"Humph. Well, it never worked, anyway. I've always handled a story my way. Not his." Her eyes widened as another thought struck her. "Think about it, Larkin. You could trade me in for a pocket full of cash. Isn't that tempting?"

Oddly enough, the idea of handing Blossom over to anyone didn't appeal to him at all. Money meant nothing to him. It never had. But that greeting she'd given him a few minutes ago—that had affected him far more than a pocket full of money. In fact, his mind was still wrestling with the warm, tender feelings her bear hug had given him.

"I'm not interested in money," he answered.

She thought about that for a few seconds, then a sly smile tilted her pink lips. "But you're interested in me?"

Once again he was taken aback by her forwardness. "I do believe you'd ask a fella anything," he said with dismay.

Blossom shook her head. "Not *any* fella. And not *anything*. Besides, it would be rather hypocritical of me to be closemouthed, then get on television and talk about other people's private lives."

Intrigued by her reasoning, he folded his arms

against his chest, then asked, "Why do you discuss other people's private lives?"

Glancing away from him, she focused on the coal oil lamp pushed to one side of the table. Today while she'd been waiting for his return, she'd washed the soot from the globe. Tonight, when they ate supper, she'd be able to see his face.

"Because it's my job," she answered.

"You certainly do it thoroughly."

"I wouldn't do any job halfway. I'm just not that sort of person," she said proudly.

"Do you like what you do?"

That brought her chin up and Luke could see a mixture of pride and confusion on her features.

"Look, I can't help it that people get themselves into scandalous messes. If they don't want their behavior aired to the public, they shouldn't be doing what they're doing."

"You think it's that simple, do you? That everyone can control themselves at all times and in every situation?" He made a grunting noise of disbelief. "You're obviously too young to understand what it means to be human."

Her mouth open, Blossom watched him rise from the table and go over to the kitchen area.

"If you think I've always had things easy, you're crazy," she shot back at him.

Then before he had a chance to reply, she jumped up from her seat and went to stand beside him at the counter. He met her mutinous face with raised brows.

Heaving out a breath, she said, "While I was growing up, my mother flitted from one man to the next. I never knew where we were going to be living. Through the years my father sent a few dollars to help out, but only when the mood hit him. I've never been able to rely on my parents for any sort of steady support, and I decided early on that once I was grown, I would do better. I managed to get my associate degree in communications and then I followed Chelsea Markum around learning the ropes of the business—the hard way. I was determined to succeed at this job—at this chance to make something of myself. And I have. If that makes me inhuman, then so be it!''

He'd touched on a nerve. That much was obvious. Her blue eyes were blazing up at him, her chin was tilted to a stubborn angle. Luke was sorely tempted to kiss her. To prove a point and to quench the fire of wanting her.

''I never accused you of being lazy or lacking ambition,'' he reasoned.

''No. You accused me of something much worse. You implied that I was insensitive, that I wasn't capable of showing compassion or understanding. I'm not a hard person, Larkin. I just have to give that impression in order to do my job. I have to—to steel myself against being soft. Like a nurse is forced to do in order to help a patient. I—''

Her words halted as frustration overtook her, then before Luke could utter a word, she turned and hurried out of the cabin. Grimly, he watched the screen door bang shut behind her.

Luke didn't know that much about women. His encounters with the opposite sex over the years had been brief. He'd never had a companion long enough to learn about her ethics or moods, or her goals in life and how she would go about getting them. Yet he understood basic human nature, and he'd have to be blind and deaf not to see that Blossom was desperately wanting him to recognize her hard-won achievements.

But did he want to involve himself in her feelings, her wants and needs? No! He'd be a fool to let himself. Yet when she'd talked about steeling herself in order to do her job, she'd touched a place deep inside him. He knew all about hardening his heart in order to survive. And because he knew, he wanted to spare this beautiful young woman the scars he'd acquired from living such a cynical existence.

Wiping a weary hand over his face, he walked out to the front porch.

She was sitting on the east end with her back to him. Her head was bent forward and the thick blond ponytail at the back of her head fell in tangles over her left shoulder. As Luke took a seat beside her, he had to fight the urge to push his hand into the silky mass and twine it around his fingers.

"What are you doing out here?" she mumbled crossly.

"I could ask the same of you," he said quietly.

She drew in a deep breath, then released it with a sigh. "I don't like being angry."

Funny, but Luke had never given a damn who he made angry. He spoke his mind and to hell with anyone who didn't agree. Yet he hated the idea that he'd somehow disappointed this woman.

"And I suppose I made you angry?"

She scuffed her bare toes against the dirt and pebbles beneath her feet. "For a few moments," she admitted. "But it's passed. I realize it was stupid of me to think you would understand anything about what I do or why."

Even though she was looking away from him, he could see enough of her profile to see that her features were gripped with a sad sort of resignation. Luke found himself wanting to reach out and slide his fingers along her jaw. He wanted to see her smile at him, the same way she had when he'd arrived a few minutes ago.

He cleared his throat, then said quietly, "I understand a whole lot more than you think, Blossom."

Mocking disbelief marred her features as she turned to look at him. "How could you? You think my job is superficial."

"Maybe I do think it's shallow and not up to your potential. But I can see that you don't feel that way about it. And I can also see that in order for you to do your job, you have to be someone you aren't."

As she listened to what he was saying, her forehead wrinkled with confusion. She'd never thought of her job in that way before and the revelation bothered her. "I didn't say I had to be someone else," she corrected him. "I said I had to make myself hard at times—but—"

She stopped as his hand reached out and settled over her forearm. "You're making a mistake, Blossom. Take my word for it."

Her brows shot up. "Making a mistake? How—"

"You think I don't understand how you feel. But I do, Blossom. I know what it's like to harden your heart to life's ugliness—just to survive your job. I know that it ruins a person. It's ruined me."

His words disturbed her, but not nearly as much as the heat of his fingers pressing into her flesh. She wanted those same hands to touch her all over, to hold her close against him. She wanted to lean her face into his until their lips met and she was tasting the rich, sultry magic of his kiss.

"You—don't looked ruined to me," she whispered.

One side of his mouth crooked upward. "Last night you wanted to kill me."

Her warm gaze slid slowly, longingly over the rough angles and planes of his face. "Last night I didn't know you," she reasoned.

His features suddenly hardened as he tried to fight the pull of her blue eyes and moist lips. "You don't know me now."

Sensing that he was retreating from her, she scooted closer and reached for his hand. When she slid her fingers between his, she saw him swallow as though the connection was more intimate than a kiss. And maybe it was to a man like him, she thought.

"Yes, I do."

He breathed deeply as the need to take her into his arms warred with the sensible part of him. "You little fool," he murmured. "You're too young—"

"I may be young," she interrupted. "But I'm not a fool. I've got a lot more street smarts than you give me credit for. I've known all along that you've been lying to me."

Everything inside him went still. "Lying about what?"

"Who you are and what you are."

He swallowed once again as her fingers tightened on his. "If you know so much, then who am I?"

A smile suddenly spread across her face and Luke felt the fool in him melt like a chunk of ice on hot pavement.

"It doesn't matter who you are," she answered. "I trust you."

Down through the years Luke had found himself in some tight spots, some that could even have cost him his life. Yet he'd never been as afraid as he was at this moment. For it was quickly dawning on him that Blossom was not like any woman who'd ever been in his life before. When she touched him, looked at him, talked to him, he wasn't just seeing a beautiful female who could ease his sexual urges. He was seeing a spirit, a personality, who for the first time in his life made him want to be a normal man with an everyday life and a woman to love him.

Feeling the sudden need for oxygen, he breathed in deeply, but all he managed to draw in was the flowery scent of her skin and hair.

"You shouldn't be trusting me, Blossom."

"I shouldn't be doing this, either, but I want to," she reasoned, then before he could duck or dodge, she slid her arms around his neck and pressed her lips against his.

Luke couldn't resist the warm honey taste of her lips any more than he could stop breathing. Forgetting everything but the incessant need to have her, he pulled her across his lap and deepened the kiss.

Moved by his needy response, Blossom opened her mouth to him and met the invasion of his tongue with a blissful groan. His hands roamed her back, her waist and finally her breasts.

Eventually the craving to feel her skin had his hands dipping beneath the hem of the T-shirt she was wearing.

With his lips still feasting on hers, he released the clasp of her bra, then beneath the loosened fabric, he cupped his hand around one naked breast. Blossom's cry of pleasure was immediately swallowed up by another hungry kiss.

Blood pounded through his veins, fired his loins and blotted out what little bit of rationality he'd been hanging on to. Urgently, he eased her down onto the floor of the porch and pushed up the shirt to expose one perfect breast to his view.

With a thumb and forefinger, he teased the nipple rigid, then dipped his head and laved it with his tongue. As she lay beneath him, Blossom's senses were whirling with a desire so strong it was blotting out everything, including where they were and the danger that could have followed him back here to the cabin. She'd never wanted anything in her life as much as she wanted this man. And somewhere in the trembling touch of his hands and the desperate search of his lips, she felt he wanted and needed her just as badly.

Just off to their left, at the edge of the woods, a mourning dove pierced the quietness of the evening. The plaintive sound echoed the yearning in Blossom's heart and she wrapped her arms even more tightly around him.

"Oh, Larkin, make love to me. Here. Now," she pleaded.

Chapter Five

The huskily spoken invitation did more than anything to cool Luke's heated senses. He couldn't make love to this woman, he argued with himself. She was too young. And in spite of what she'd said, too innocent as to who and what he really was. Though she was partly to blame, he'd gotten her into this dangerous predicament. He'd never forgive himself if he took advantage of her while she was dependent on him.

Slowly, he pulled down her clothing and eased away from her. "Come on," he said firmly. "Let's go have our supper."

Still flushed and breathless from his ardent attention, she rose to a sitting position and stared at him. "Just like that?" she asked with disbelief.

He grimaced. "Yeah. Just like that."

Her eyes widened as an empty spot grew larger and larger inside her. "But what about—"

"Forget about it," he snapped. "It's not going to happen. Now or ever."

Moisture flooded her eyes, but Luke did as he'd always had to do. He hardened himself to the sight. She would be better off for his rejection, he told himself. Later, she would thank him for saving her from the embarrassment of making love to a man like him. A man who never really gave anything of himself to anyone. Because he had nothing to give.

Rising to a standing position, he reached down and pulled her to her feet. "Don't go soft on me now, Blossom. Do it later, when I'm gone."

She didn't understand his words any more than she understood the abrupt change in him. Even now as he declared that nothing was going to happen between them, she could see a low fire banked in his eyes.

"You want to make love to me. I know you do," she said as though he needed to be reminded.

"I never said I didn't. I said it wasn't going to happen. And don't ask me why. That part of it doesn't matter. Just be glad I had sense enough to stop when I did."

"Then you—" She stopped, her expression wounded. "You would have regretted making love to me?"

If she'd been any other woman, he would have simply walked away. He'd never felt the need or obligation to explain himself to the opposite sex. That was something relegated to long-term relationships. Something he'd never had. Nor did he plan to.

Irritated more at himself than at her, he spoke gruffly. "Hell, yes, Blossom! I'm several years older than you. Besides that, I'm a hard-nosed bastard. Not the sort you need to get tangled in the sheets with."

She blushed at his frankness, then to his great surprise, she tilted her head to one side and regarded him with a smile that turned his insides to jelly.

"Why, Larkin, I do believe you have a conscience."

He frowned at her. "And that makes you happy?"

She looped her arm through his, then with her free arm pushed open the screen door. "Of course. It tells me you care."

Luke was smart enough to know when to keep his mouth shut, and this was one of those times. Thankfully, Blossom didn't push him for a response. She seemed to sense that they both needed to put the episode on the porch behind them, at least for now.

Once inside the house, she moved away from him. At the cabinets she began to sort through the assortment of cans he'd placed there.

"What did you want to eat?" she asked.

"Tamales, stew or sardines," he answered. "You choose. It doesn't matter to me."

She picked up a fat can of tamales. "I love these things when they're fresh. But beggars can't be choosers."

Walking over to her, he plucked the can from her hands. "Let me open this while you find a pot to heat them in," he told her.

For the next few minutes they worked together in the kitchen preparing the simple meal. As they exchanged minimal words, Luke was careful to keep a safe distance between them. But even so, he was acutely aware of her warm, tempting body moving around the small workspace. More than once, he caught himself wondering how it might be if the two of them had come here together under different circumstances. Like on a lovers' getaway. Or a secluded honeymoon. The idea of making love to her at his leisure was enough to make him crazy.

"So," she said, once they took their seats at the small table. "You haven't told me what you accomplished in Austin."

While they'd been preparing the meal, the sun had disappeared and the cabin had grown gloomy. A few moments ago, Larkin had lit the coal oil lamp and now the yellow glow flickered warmly across his face.

"Not much. You read it."

She held her plate out for a helping of tamales. While he carefully spooned the steaming food for her, she said, "The paper didn't tell us much more than we already knew. Except that no one has been apprehended."

He served himself a hefty portion of tamales. "Unfortunately, that's true," he admitted. "And also that there's a reward out for your safe return."

She laughed as she tore into a package of tortilla chips. "Right now, I'd love to be a fly on the wall of the television studio."

"Eavesdroppers very seldom hear good things about themselves."

"That's true." Dimples continued to come and go in her cheeks. Watching her, Luke realized he would like to kiss both indented spots before moving on to the moist curve of her lips. "But don't you sometimes wonder," she continued, "what people might say about you if you were dead and gone?"

According to the authorities back on the West Coast, who'd placed Luke in the Witness Security Program, he was already dead and gone. The people he'd worked with, his brother and sisters, and what few acquaintances he'd had, would never likely see him again. Unless something could be done about the Patriots for Purity. And so far not one government security agency had been able to find the small radical group, much less stop them from tracking him.

"If people want to talk about me, I'd prefer they do it to my face while I'm still alive."

She chuckled again. "Most people aren't that brave. The slurs come later when a person is not around to defend himself."

"From what the paper said, the authorities didn't imply that they think you're dead," he pointed out.

She snorted. "Like you said, the authorities aren't talking to the press. Now, if you had taken me with you today I could have done some real investigating. I have connections, you know. Particularly with the police. But don't tell anyone. I don't want to lose my two sources."

His brows lifted. "Men, no doubt. I'm not going to ask how you repay them for the favors," he said with a disgusted shake of his head.

She shot him an indignant look. "I repay them with a thank-you. And sometimes I'm lucky enough to pick up information that might help them on unsolved cases. When that happens, I pass it on to them. Unlike you, they appreciate my investigative skills."

Luke had known for some time that she'd been using those investigative skills of hers to track him down. Like her, he had friends in high places, too. The man who owned the cabin, for instance, was a Texas Ranger whom he'd once helped years ago was now stationed in Austin and had alerted Luke to the fact that Blossom Woodward had been asking questions around town about him. Concerned as to what she might unearth about him and his battle with the Patriots of Purity, he'd immediately set out to Austin to observe her movements. It wasn't until he'd taken the job at the clinic that he learned his brother and sister were also in town. Now, because of Blossom, Luke had unknowingly brought danger to them and all of the Maitlands.

"Larkin, are you listening to me?"

Her question broke into his wandering thoughts, and he realized he'd been gone from their conversation for several moments.

"Did you say something else?" he asked.

Rolling her eyes, she repeated, "I was saying that it's obvious nothing has changed since yesterday. What do you plan to do? Just stay here until the police catch the gunmen?"

He chewed a piece of mushy tamale, then swallowed. "I guess there could be worse things than growing old and gray in this cabin. But I'm not going to wait around and find out what they are."

She looked at him, her fork paused in midair. "What do you mean? Do you think it's safe and we can go back now?"

His frown was mocking. "Going back to Austin now would be like stepping into a pen full of Spanish bulls. There's no way in hell we can go back to life as usual."

Of course he was going to say that, she thought. Otherwise, he would have never taken the trouble to bring food back with him.

"Okay, if that's true, then what are we going to do?"

"Forget the 'we,' honey. I'm going after them myself."

The grim implication of his words sent a chill crawling up Blossom's spine.

After a few thoughtful bites, she asked, "And how do you propose to do that? You don't know where these people are any more than the police do. If a whole team of men can't find them, what makes you think one single man could manage it?"

His smooth expression didn't alter, and Blossom found herself thinking that he could make a killing at poker. No one would be able to tell whether he was holding four aces or a mixed hand.

"Blossom, you're jumping the gun in thinking I'm going out hunting for the shooters. That would be fruitless. I'm going to make them come to me."

Her mouth parted as she continued to stare at him. "Are you crazy, Larkin? You think you can just get on a tailgate and call them up like a herd of cattle?"

Ignoring her sarcasm, he continued to shovel food into his mouth. "No. I'm going to set a trap for them. And once they're in it, I'll turn them over to the police."

The resolution in his voice terrified Blossom. Tossing down her fork, she grabbed his forearm. "You'd be insane to try to do something like that by yourself. Promise me you'll call the police before you ever try such a thing! Promise me!"

As Luke looked into her pleading blue eyes, he wished he could promise her anything and everything to make her happy, to make her see him as a man worthy of her attention, her love. But he was in no position to be promising a woman anything. And even if things were different, he wasn't the right sort of man for Blossom Woodward. She was young and fresh and just starting her life. He'd seen too much of the bad to be able to give lasting happiness to anyone. Even himself.

"No, Blossom. I'm not about to let the police in on this thing. If—"

"But why?" she cut in. "Are you trying to get yourself killed?"

He shook his head. "You've been telling me how good you are at your work, so think about it, Blossom. A show of uniformed officers would scare the gunmen off before anyone had a chance to get a hand on them. They'd only come sneaking back and strike when least expected. No. I'm going to do this my own way."

Her shoulders sagged as she accepted his reasoning. "Okay. So you're probably right about the police. But, still, to set a trap you have to have some sort of bait. We don't know what these maniacs want. If it's Megan—"

"It isn't her."

Blossom motioned with her head to the newspaper lying on the couch behind them. "That's not what the press says."

"The press is in the dark," he said sharply. "They'll come after me. All I have to do is give them a chance."

He was frightening her more and more. Not simply because he had this fool, heroic notion of catching the assailants by himself. It was his clipped replies and the certainty of his attitude that was really chilling her. Like she'd told him before, she might be young, but she was also street-smart. And it was becoming very clear to her that Larkin knew exactly who these gunmen were and what they wanted. Him.

But why, she wondered. If there was any way she was going to be able to help him, she had to know.

Unwittingly, she crept her hand up his arm until it was resting on his shoulder. "How do you know these men will come after you? What are you not telling me, Larkin?"

"I've told you everything you need to know," he said, then pointed his fork toward her plate. "Your food is getting cold. Eat."

"How do you expect me to eat after you spring this suicidal plan of yours on me—then refuse to explain what it's all about?"

"You just told me you were hungry. And as for this plan—you already know everything about it that you need to know."

She groaned with frustration. "You know who these men are, don't you? You know that they're after you. Why?"

"I'm not one of your subjects on *Tattle Today TV*, Blossom. So drop it!"

Crushed by his cutting retort, Blossom removed her hand from his shoulder and turned back to her food. As she forced several bites down her throat, she told herself she'd been a fool to let herself think their little interlude on the porch had meant anything to him. She'd scooted close and he'd gotten randy. That's all there had been to the whole thing.

What do you expect, Blossom, the man believes you'd trade your own grandmother for a good story. Even if he wanted to share the private part of his life with you, he probably wouldn't. Because he can't trust you. He knows you've exposed too many people in the past that didn't want to be exposed. And he believes you'd do the same thing to him.

From the corner of her eye she watched him fork the last of the food into his mouth. His expression was rigid, his thoughts purposely closed off to her.

He was so wrong about her. She had to make him, see that. But something told her that all the arguing, all the promises and reassurances she might make to him wouldn't be enough to earn his trust. She would have to gain that some other way. But how long would that take? she wondered. Even worse, would it be too late?

"You're wrong about me, you know," she said quietly.

He looked at her as though he dared her to say more.

She took a deep breath, then released it with a ragged sigh. "It's true that I report gossip. But I'm not a gossiper. I don't tell anything that's been spoken to me in confidence. I would never betray my friends—or anyone I'm close to—in such a way."

Was she trying to tell him that she considered herself close to him? Luke asked himself. If she was, he didn't want to hear it. Yesterday, he'd complicated his predicament by bringing her along with him. Granted, he didn't have much choice in the matter. But since then he'd made a damn mess of things by not keeping a cool distance. Instead he'd wound up kissing her several times. Or she'd wound up kissing him. Either way was an invitation to trouble.

"You're like the little boy who cried wolf one too many times, Blossom. I watched you in action around the clinic. You're like a bulldozer, pushing your way over people to get inside the Maitland family."

"That's because—"

"It's your job," he finished for her.

She made a palms-up gesture. "Yes. They're one of the most important, prominent families in Austin. The public wants to hear about them."

"And you believe giving the public what it wants makes doing what you do okay."

"Well—it's—oh, there's no use in this. We've already been through it." With a toss of her head, she got up from the table. "Go ahead and keep everything to yourself. You don't have to tell me anything. But when you…get yourself killed…I don't want to be around to see it."

Her choked words were immediately followed by the slamming of the screen door, then total silence.

Luke closed his eyes and wiped a weary hand over his face. He'd never needed or wanted to trust a woman. So why, of all people, did he desperately want to believe Blossom Woodward?

Cursing because he didn't like the answer, he rose to his feet and began to clear away the remnants of their supper.

Outside, Blossom swatted at the mosquito buzzing in front of her face. For the past hour the hungry pest had made a feast of her bare arms and feet, not to mention a few nips on her neck. Yet in spite of her discomfort, she was loathe to go back inside the cabin. Being that close to Larkin was something she wasn't up to yet. The man stirred her. Not just in physical ways, but other ways, too. Even when he was freezing her out, she wanted to put her arms around him, to reassure him that he wasn't alone.

With her chin resting on the heel of her palm, she mulled over that last thought. Why she had the notion that Larkin was a man alone, she didn't know. He could have a big, loving family somewhere here in Texas or parts beyond.

But he didn't, she thought, continuing her musings. She'd always had a knack for reading people, and her job had succeeded in making her even better at summing up people. Larkin was not a family man. Not a husband. Not a father. And from what little he'd said about his parents, they were out of his life, too. He was a loner, all right, and he was hiding something from her. Maybe he was even trying to hide a few things from himself.

Her gaze strayed eastward, to where a half moon was creeping up over the treetops. The fingers of silver light filtering through the branches illuminated the open area in front of the cabin. With her eyes already adjusted to the darkness, Blossom could easily discern where the road started into the woods.

There was nothing stopping her from getting up and walking away. The moon would be up for several hours, providing enough light for her to avoid any rattlesnakes or other deadly wildlife prowling the road. Blossom wasn't a timid person. She wasn't afraid to attempt the trek out of here. She simply didn't want to leave. Not without Larkin.

Glancing over her shoulder, she could see the dim glow of the coal oil lamp on the table, but there was no sign of him. She wondered what he was thinking and why she should care.

Because you have that sickness, Blossom. That thing some people get after they've been held prisoner for a while. Their sympathy gets misguided and goes to their captor.

She silently snorted at the voice going off in her head. She wasn't a prisoner and it wasn't sympathy she was feeling toward Larkin. Not by a long shot. Anger, passion, desire, the need to keep him safe. He elicited all those things from her and more. He'd become important to her. Not as a story, but as a man. And she didn't know what to do about her new feelings.

The screen door banged softly, the sound only slightly louder than the chaotic chorus of frogs, crickets and other night creatures inhabiting the woods around them. As he took a seat beside her, Blossom couldn't stop her heart from swelling with gladness.

"You've been out here a long time," he said.

One shoulder scrunched upward toward her ear. "There's nothing else to do. And it's too early to go to bed."

Since their small supper, nearly two hours had passed. Luke had spent most of that time assuring himself he didn't want to talk to Blossom. The minute he opened his mouth, she wanted to ask more. Even so, the desire to be near her, to hear her voice, had eventually become too strong for him to resist. Now here he was fighting with himself to keep his hands off her and his mouth shut.

"What are you doing out here?" she asked bluntly.

"Actually, I've been thinking things over, Blossom. So far you've been asking me all the questions. I've decided it's time I asked you a few."

Chapter Six

Surprise widened her eyes, then slowly a smug smile spread across her lips as though she was confident she could answer any question he might toss her way.

"Okay. Shoot. What would you like to know? I'll give you the basics," she said before he could respond. "I was born in Texas twenty-one years ago. I've never been married but someday I'd like to be. I've never had a child, but eventually I'd like to have several."

He couldn't imagine this sassy sexpot wanting to be the mother of one child, much less several. Perhaps there was much more of her that she kept hidden from the public and the camera's eye than he'd first thought.

"Several?"

"Yes," she answered. "I hated being an only child. I still do. Children need siblings. Not just for playmates while they're growing up, but for love and support through all their years. I've never had, nor ever will have either of those things. What about you?"

Luke thought about his own brother and sisters. He'd not seen them in years. Once he'd reached eighteen he'd left home. Not that the place had been a home in the normal sense of the word. The ratty apartment where Veronica had housed her four children had been just a place to shelter and feed them. When Luke and his siblings had been small, they'd all been close to one another. Clinging together for support in a harsh, uncertain world. But later, as adults, three of them—Luke, Rafe and Laura—had all gone their separate ways, each leaving Las Vegas with the desire to find a better life and to put all the bad memories of their childhood behind them. Only Janelle had chosen to stay behind and follow in their parents' footsteps. And from all the stories Luke had been hearing about her, she'd done a bang-up job of becoming a loser.

Shaking away that dour thought, he said to Blossom, "I'm supposed to be asking the questions, remember?"

"Sorry," she replied with a sheepish grin. "It's just an occupational habit of mine. I can't help myself."

"So I've noticed," he said wryly, then because he felt an odd stab of guilt, he could no longer look at her face and his gaze drifted to her feet. In spite of his earlier warnings to keep her shoes on, they were still bare. A deep, shocking pink had been painted on her toenails, and he wondered if she was one of those women who liked to run around the house barefoot, or partially naked. She didn't seem the sort to have inhibitions. At least not with him. But what about when she was alone, or with some other man? he wondered. No. He didn't want to think about some other man with Blossom. Not in that way.

"I thought you were going to ask me something," she reminded him after several silent moments had passed.

"Nothing earth-shaking. I've just been thinking about this whole Maitland thing you've been working on. The talk around the clinic is that you've been hunting another family member—a Luke Maitland. What's the reason?"

"You heard right," she told him. "I've been hunting Luke for nearly three months now. And so far I've come up against a blank wall. I don't know how any one person could keep his identity so well hidden."

Feigning a casualness he was far from feeling, he rested his elbows on his knees and allowed his hands to drop between his legs. "How do you know he's trying to keep it hidden?"

Sighing, she reached up and tugged the rubber band from her hair. The blond locks tumbled onto her shoulders, instantly transforming her appearance from innocent to seductive.

Scrubbing her fingers against her scalp where the ponytail had been affixed to her head, she answered, "Because I've been running up against too many barriers. No matter what source I've tried, I keep coming up with the same response. They have no record of Luke Maitland. It's like the man doesn't exist. Even my cop connections haven't been able to help me."

The tense coil inside Luke eased somewhat. Apparently the Witness Security Program had been working, for the most part. How had the Liberators tracked him? He didn't know. He suspected that the

Maitlands' troubles had made the newspapers one too many times. The radicals had probably spotted one of the articles, put two and two together and come to Austin on the hunch that Luke was connected to the rich family and might be somewhere in the vicinity.

But that was an altogether different question. For weeks now, he'd wanted to know why finding Luke Maitland was so important to this woman. What was she going to gain from finding him?

"Maybe the man doesn't exist," he ventured.

She groaned loudly. "Oh, please. Megan Maitland is a highly intelligent woman. She wouldn't send feelers out for her long-lost relatives if they didn't exist."

"Feelers?"

Blossom rubbed the back of her arms to ward off any nearby mosquitoes. "Oh, you know—" she stopped, shook her head, then started again. "Maybe you don't. Maybe I should start at the beginning."

"That's usually the best place," he agreed.

She searched his face for a hint of sarcasm, but oddly enough there was none to be seen. Encouraged by his interest in a story she'd lived and breathed for the past several months, she began to relate the facts in abbreviated form.

"Well, Megan had a brother-in-law, Robert Maitland, who was pretty much the black sheep of the family. Seems he skipped out years ago right after his wife was killed in a car accident. He dumped his two kids, Anna and R.J., on his older brother William, took his part of the Maitland inheritance, and lit out for parts unknown. That was close to thirty-eight years ago. Now fastforward to the present. Megan's baby grandson, Chase, was recently kidnapped, and it turned out that the mastermind behind the whole thing was Robert's daughter, Janelle Maitland Jones. After the dust settled over all that hullabaloo, Megan found out she had more relatives that she didn't know about. Robert had another daughter and two sons, and R.J. and Anna had brothers and another sister they'd never met."

Luke stared at her as his mind whirled. R.J. and Anna were his half siblings! The fact that his father had deserted two other children here in Austin before his life in Las Vegas wasn't all that surprising. The man had been scum. The only person Robert Maitland had ever cared about was Robert Maitland. But the sudden news that he had a brother and sister he'd never met left him with a very strange feeling, one that he hoped didn't show on his face.

"I wonder what they—" he murmured, then realizing he was thinking out loud, he quickly collected himself and glanced at Blossom. "R.J. and Anna," he continued, "what do they think about all this? About Megan dragging in brothers and sisters they didn't know about? They might not appreciate having newly discovered siblings thrown at them."

She seemed to regard his remark with curiosity, and Luke wished liked hell he'd never said it. But it was too late to take it back. Too late for a lot of things, he thought dismally.

She made a dismissive gesture with her hand. "As far as I can gather, R.J. and Anna get on with Rafe and Laura very well. It appears that they're all happy to have found one another. But Luke seems to be a different matter with the family."

Luke froze. What did that mean? he wondered. Furthermore, should he risk asking her?

He had to, he realized. Though Blossom didn't

know it, she was discussing his life. Whether she
learned his real identity later on depended on many
things. The main one being whether he managed to
stay alive.

"What does that mean?"

"Well, from what all my little birds tell me, it turns
out that Rafe and Laura aren't anything like their sin-
ister sister Janelle. But no one knows about Luke. I've
heard Megan is worried that he and Janelle might be
in cahoots and that she might have put him up to
sabotaging the clinic for revenge."

So, even without knowing anything about him or
ever meeting him, Megan and her family suspected
him of being as ruthless and greedy as Robert. Maybe
that shouldn't come as a surprise after all that Janelle
had done to them. Not counting what Robert had done
in the past. Still, the idea that the Maitland family
considered Luke's morals questionable hurt him far
more than it should have. He'd spent years trying to
rise above the dark shadow of his father, but it looked
as though Robert's reputation was still haunting him.
And it certainly didn't help matters that Janelle had
turned out rotten to the core. Her crime against the
Maitlands had been one of the first things he'd
learned about after arriving in Austin.

"I thought Janelle was in prison," he said.

"She is now. She had escaped for a time. But a
few weeks ago she was captured and sent back to
serve the rest of her sentence," Blossom told him.
"So you can see why Megan must be nervous. I just
wonder what she's been thinking since the shooting.
The Maitland mansion is probably swarming with security guards."

Luke hoped guards were crawling all over the

place. If the Liberators had tracked him to the Maitland clinic, they wouldn't stop there. Even at this moment they could be planning to infiltrate the mansion in an effort to find Luke. He couldn't let that happen. If any of the Maitlands were harmed because of him, he couldn't live with himself.

"Of course there's also the notion floating around that Hugh Blake is up to no good, too."

Blossom's added information interrupted Luke's thoughts and he looked at her with blank surprise. Since he'd gone to work at the clinic as a way of picking up information about Blossom Woodward and her efforts to find Luke Maitland, he'd learned about many of the people who worked there. For the life of him, he couldn't imagine the man Blossom had just mentioned as being anything but honest and aboveboard.

"Hugh Blake?" he echoed. "The older man—the attorney for Maitland Maternity? Megan and her family think he might be the one who's been doing the damaging mischief at the clinic?"

Frowning, Blossom nodded. "Well, some of the sabotage was done in such a way as to make Hugh look mighty suspicious. But frankly, where Hugh is concerned, I believe the Maitlands are barking up the wrong tree."

Luke was inclined to agree with her. Still, he wanted to know why Blossom thought so. "How did you come to that conclusion?"

"I don't have any facts or proof," she admitted. "Just my feminine instinct. Besides, from what I can gather, the man is plainly smitten with Megan. He wouldn't do anything to hurt the woman."

"Are the two of them sweethearts?"

Blossom smiled at his use of the old-fashioned term because it hinted at something she'd suspected all along. Deep down, Larkin was a romantic guy. He was just too busy being tough to know it.

"No. Not officially. Hugh's going to have to get Clyde Mitchum out of the picture before that could ever happen." She shook her head with disgust. "I can't imagine why Megan would allow that man back in her life. When she was only seventeen, he got her pregnant, then dumped her. How could a woman forgive or forget that? Maybe he has changed as he claims, but I wouldn't trust him as far as I could throw him."

Luke studied Blossom's rigid profile. For the most part she appeared to be a free, innocent spirit. But there were other times, like this one, when he could see a hard, cynical streak guiding her thinking and motivation. He wondered if having irresponsible parents or a half-shady job was to blame.

"I don't know the guy, but the newspaper quoted Megan as saying that Clyde was a hero. That he'd saved her and Chase's life by throwing himself in front of them when the bullets were fired," Luke pointed out.

Blossom mulled over Luke's words, then her gaze slanted over to his face. The corners of her lips tilted ever so slightly upward as she replied, "If that's the case, then you're certainly my hero."

At the same time, nearly forty miles away in the Maitland mansion in Austin, Megan was trying her best to concentrate on a stack of backlogged work, but so far was having little success. Yesterday's shooting had shaken her far more than she'd led the rest of the family to believe. The loud popping explosions of the guns and the terrified screams of the people outside the clinic were still ringing in her ears. Every few minutes she had to stop and remind herself that her little grandson, Chase, was safe. But for how long? she wondered. Which member of her family would be the next target?

A light knock sounded on the heavy wooden door to her office. Megan looked tensely up from the document she'd been trying to read.

"Yes, come in," she invited.

At the sight of Clyde Mitchum stepping through the door, the older woman visibly relaxed.

"I know I'm bothering you, Megan, but can you spare me a few minutes?" he asked.

Smiling, she put her pen aside and leaned comfortably back in the leather office chair. Around them, the classic, tasteful furnishings interspersed with family photos and other sentimental objects expressed Megan's strong personality.

She said, "I'm glad it's you, Clyde. It gives me the chance to privately thank you for what you did yesterday. If not for you, Chase and I might be dead now."

Clearly bothered by the woman's praise, Clyde took a seat in front of her desk, then proceeded to shake his head. "I'm not a hero, Megan. Please don't try to make me out as one."

Smiling wanly, she said, "This isn't the time for you to be humble, Clyde. I—"

His expression pained, he held up a hand to ward off her next words. "Megan, don't say anything more until you hear me out. This whole shooting thing has—well, I guess you could say it's woken me up to a lot of things. And frankly, I can't go on letting you—or your family—think I'm a hero,'' he said in a voice hoarse with remorse. ''You might as well know I'm a fraud, Megan. I didn't just come here to Austin to make amends with you. I...''

His words trailed away as he stared at the floor. Puzzled by his attitude, Megan finished the sentence for him. ''I understand you also wanted to get to know your son, Connor.''

With nervous agitation, Clyde rubbed his hands against his thighs. ''Well—'' He stopped, sighed heavily, then shook his head. ''Getting to know you and Connor and the whole Maitland family has been more than I bargained for. Yesterday when those bullets were fired, I realized how very much all of you meant to me. I realized how lucky I was to have found my son. But now—through my own selfishness I'm probably going to lose you all.''

For long moments she studied his troubled face. ''What are you trying to tell me, Clyde?''

He drew in a long breath, then huffed it out. ''I'm the one who caused the fire and—all the other bad accidents at the clinic.''

Megan gasped with shock, then shook her head with bitter disbelief. Long, tense moments passed before she was finally able to speak. ''Why, Clyde? I was certain you felt like you're a part of this family. Am I wrong? The same way I was wrong about Janelle?''

Urgently, he went around Megan's desk and kneeled humbly in front of her chair. ''You're not wrong, Megan. That's why I had to confess. You, Connor and the whole family have made me see there're much more important things than…money," he added shamefully.

She looked perplexed. "Money? That's what this is all about? I don't understand. All those accidents— how did you expect to gain anything—"

"Hugh," he interrupted. "I could see that he and you were…well, if the two of you wound up getting married, you'd forget all about me. So I decided my only chance was to try to make him look bad in your eyes."

Megan groaned aloud. "Oh, Clyde, I don't—"

Before she could go on, he clutched both her hands between his. "Forgive me, Megan. I realize it's a lot to ask. But I have sincerely changed. And if you'll give me the chance, I'll make it up to you. I'll try to help in every way I can to find the gunmen who shot at us yesterday."

"Then the incident yesterday had nothing to do with the other mishaps at the clinic," she said with sudden understanding.

He looked at her desperately. "No. That's why the shooting shook the ground beneath my feet, Megan. Someone really is out for Maitland blood. And we have to find them before that happens. Can you and the rest of the family forgive me enough to allow me to help?"

Clyde was by no means perfect, but at least he was being honest with her, Megan thought. Most of all, when danger was near, he'd put her and Chase's safety before his own, which to her more than proved he was a changed man.

She rose to her feet. "I've already forgiven you, Clyde," she said with a resigned smile. "And I'm sure the rest of the family will feel the same as I do. Why don't we go ask them?''

Clyde gratefully squeezed her hands. ''You're one of a kind, Megan.''

Back at the cabin, Luke wasn't at all sure how to take Blossom's praise. He'd never been called a hero before. Certainly not by a beautiful woman. He tried to tell himself she'd meant it in a teasing way. Yet he couldn't ignore the serious light in her eyes, any more than he could dismiss the slow, earnest thud of his heart.

''Blossom, your thinking is misguided.''

''Hmm. Maybe. But I don't think so.''

''I've been called everything but a hero. The word doesn't fit me,'' he told her.

The tiny smile that spread across her lips was a bit secretive, even provocative. Luke felt himself drawn to it and the warm nearness of her body.

''I'm the one in a position to judge that,'' she said. ''Not you.''

He tried to laugh, but the strange pressure around his heart kept him from it. In search of relief, he wiped a hand over his face, then looked out at the moonstruck night.

''Uh—I was asking you before about Luke Maitland,'' he said quietly. ''I'm getting the impression that you're trying to find the man because you believe he's the one behind all the Maitland troubles.''

She shifted slightly and her shoulder pressed warmly against his. The touch brought Luke's head around and he instantly found himself staring straight into her blue eyes.

''Your impression is wrong,'' she said. ''So far I

haven't found any sort of evidence to that effect. The only thing I can unearth about Luke is that he's missing. That's why searching for him has become my number one priority. He's the elusive one. The one that Megan can't find. The big prize, so to speak."

And if she found him, then what? Luke wondered. She'd learn that the big prize wasn't really a prize at all, but rather a huge disappointment.

Before he could stop himself he reached for her forearm. As he began to speak, his fingers slid gently up and down the soft inner skin. "Have you ever uncovered the truth, only to find it wasn't nearly as tantalizing as the hunt?"

Her breath caught. Her lips parted. "Many times."

"Maybe this is another one of those times," he suggested.

In silent invitation, she leaned her head toward his. "No, you're wrong. Something tells me Luke Maitland is going to be worth all this effort."

Suddenly he was groaning, but whether it was from her remark or the swell of desire, he didn't know. Nor did he have time to think about it. In the next moment Blossom's hands slipped onto his shoulders; her lips lightly nibbled his.

Unable to resist, his hands speared into the thick fall of blond hair. As he deepened the kiss, his fingers mindlessly twined themselves in the silky softness.

She tasted salty and sweet and at the same time sensual and innocent. In a matter of seconds, Luke felt himself drowning in the feel of her hands tightening on his shoulders, her lips giving and giving.

Somewhere in the back of his mind, Luke knew this was more than kissing. It was a needy exchange between the two of them, a give-and-take of their most intimate selves. It would be so easy to lose himself in her, to simply surrender to all the pleasure she so willingly offered him.

And for several more moments he did, until the need for air finally parted their lips. The ragged breaths he drew deep into his lungs helped to clear the foggy desire from his brain. While he was still able to think, he gently eased her away from him.

"I think we'd better go in," he said hoarsely. "Now."

With one hand she reached out and gently cupped his jaw. Luke dared to meet her gaze and the dark desire he saw in her eyes made him inwardly groan. He didn't know why this woman wanted him. But she did. And the fact made him feel like an undeserving king.

"Why are you fighting this thing between us?" she whispered.

He couldn't keep the self-disgust he was feeling from his voice. "I don't know. Because it's damn wrong. Not to mention stupid."

Pain flickered in her eyes. "Stupid? What we just did felt stupid to you?"

No. It had felt like heaven, Luke thought. But he couldn't confess that sort of thing to her. That would be giving her hope where there was none. "Blossom, don't try to twist my words. This thing between us— whatever it is that happens when we get together— it's just physical. So don't try to make anything more of it," he ended sharply.

She shook her head. "You're only saying that because it's what you want to believe. There is more to it—"

Grabbing a hold on her shoulders, he gave her a

little shake. "We've only met. Besides that, you're too young to know what's going on, Blossom. I doubt you've ever had a serious relationship with a man."

Not to be deterred, she countered, "If you mean that I haven't had a lover, then you're right. I haven't ever slept with a man before, but I know what I'm feeling now and—"

"You're a virgin?" he interrupted swiftly, his expression one of total disbelief.

She made a palms-up gesture. "Well yes. I mean—why should that be so shocking? You just said you doubted I'd ever had a serious relationship with a man."

He stared at her while his mind reeled with the information she'd just handed him. She'd never made love to a man, yet she clearly wanted to give herself to him. He felt wildly flattered, but more than that, he was shaken. Being a virgin at her age meant she was saving herself for marriage, or at the very least for the man she loved. The notion that she was setting her sights on Luke was a problem. One he had to deal with before they both did something they'd regret.

"That's right," he admitted. "But I meant that you'd never been emotionally involved! I never dreamed you might be a virgin."

In a low, wounded voice, she said, "I realize my job might come off a bit sleazy at times and that it probably rubs off on my reputation. But like a fool, I was beginning to think you could see beyond all that. What did you think I was? A—"

He pressed his fingers against her lips before she could say the word. "What you are doesn't matter," he firmly interjected as he dropped his hand from her mouth. "It's what I'm going to do with you now that worries me."

She stared at him, her eyes wide, and then suddenly a smile tilted her lips and sparked her blue eyes. "Oh," she breathed with blissful anticipation. "Are you going to make love to me?"

Chapter Seven

"**N**o!" Luke blasted back at her.

"Why?" she countered.

Groaning with frustration, he took her by the arm and quickly led her into the house, where he promptly eased her down onto the sagging couch. The sight of her beautiful, eager face gazing up at him was very nearly his undoing.

Restlessly, he began to pace around the tiny room. "Look, Blossom, we need to get things clear right now. The two of us are not going to make love. We're not going to do *anything*. With each other, for each other, or to each other! Got that?"

She smiled at him as though she'd just found a treasure in a trunk full of junk. "Not in the least."

Luke stopped in his tracks to glare at her. "Damn it, Blossom—this situation is serious! And you—"

Before he could utter another word she left the couch and stood in front of him. Resting her palms on his chest, she said, "You're right, Larkin. It is serious. I've never felt like this about anyone before."

He shot her a look that was both skeptical and sarcastic. "You're a babe. A babe in the woods. I eat little girls like you for breakfast and spit them out before lunch. You don't have any idea what kind of hell and grief I could give you."

Undaunted by his attitude, she glided her hands up, then down the rock wall of his chest. "I'll take my chances."

He muttered a curse word under his breath.

Ignoring it, Blossom snuggled the front of her body up against his. "You know what I think? I think you're afraid of me."

"The hell you say."

Blossom smiled at his belligerent face. "It's true. You're afraid to let yourself like me. Because if you liked me, then you might get to caring. And God forbid that a man like you should care about a woman like me."

So much of what she was saying was true that he could no longer argue. The only thing he could do now was point out the folly of the two of them having any sort of relationship. It could never work.

"Okay, Blossom, you're a woman who wants information, facts and reasons. So I'm going to give them to you."

He led her back to the couch and this time took a seat beside her. Blossom immediately squared around on the cushion so that she was facing him.

"I didn't want to tell you any of this," he began ruefully, "but now it appears I don't have any choice in the matter."

Her face all serious now, she waited for him to continue.

Glancing away, Luke thrust a hand through his black hair and was immediately reminded of how long he'd been hiding himself from the Liberators, from anyone who might know and recognize him. It had been so long since he'd been himself, he sometimes wondered if he remembered how to be that man.

Sighing wearily, he continued, "It's a long story. Maybe I can sum it all up by saying I'm a phony."

His admission didn't spark even a flicker of surprise on her face. "I'm not stupid, Larkin. Like I told you before, I know that's not your real name. For some reason you're hiding."

She knew all of that and yet she still trusted him. She was either a naive fool or a woman too generous and loving for the likes of him, Luke thought.

He went on, determined to shock her into keeping her distance from him. "I know for a fact that the gunmen were after me. Not you. And not Megan or her grandson."

"I was already aware of that, too. So what are you trying to say? You were once a member of the Mafia and now they're after you for deserting the organization?"

In spite of the solemnity of the situation a rueful grin twisted his lips. "Nothing so sensational. I told you before I'm not a criminal."

"You said you worked in security. Then you have to be a cop or something close to it. Because you're the sort of man who doesn't walk down the middle of things. It's all the way with you. Good or bad."

Once again she was hitting the target, making Luke

wonder what had happened to him. He'd always been good at fooling people, but this woman seemed to have the knack of looking right through him. So far she hadn't seen enough to connect him to the elusive Luke Maitland. But she would sooner or later. When that time came, he could only hope the Liberators were already behind bars.

"I'm not a cop. I was a security agent. A specialist hired to protect high-profile people."

Her eyes intently searched his face. "Was?"

He nodded once. "Yeah," he said bitterly. "I had to…give it up. A client—a politician I'd been hired to protect—was killed in cold blood by one of my own colleagues."

Blossom gasped. "You mean a man who worked with you, who was supposed to be helping you guard this politician, did the murdering?"

Luke swallowed as the memory of that terrible incident replayed in his mind. He'd had no warning or clue that Rick Varner had gone off the deep end. The man had put up a great front right up until he'd pumped a bullet into the hard-working congressman.

"That's exactly what I'm saying. He was supposed to be laying his life on the line for the congressman. Instead, he shot him."

Blossom shook her head in disbelief, and Luke could see that this time he'd managed to shock her.

"But why?" she demanded. "And where is this killer now? Is he the one after you?"

Luke passed a weary hand over his face. Time had done nothing to lessen the guilt and helpless rage he felt over the congressman's death. "None of us in the security organization knew why Rick had suddenly turned assassin. Before the murder, he'd always been a quiet, dependable and upright man. Afterward—well he fled the crime scene, but I managed to track him down and turn him over to the California authorities. He later confessed to them and explained that he'd taken the congressman's life to help the Liberators.''

Her brows lifted in confusion. "The Liberators? Who or what are they?''

Luke grimaced. "A small militia-type group who claim they want to free the people of the United States from its oppressive government.''

"But that's crazy! Our government isn't tyrannical. We live in the most wonderful nation on this earth!''

"You and I understand that, Blossom, along with millions of others. But there are a few radicals who have a sick way of thinking. They'll stop at nothing to make headlines and try to create chaos. This particular group, whose members call themselves the Liberators, has only a handful of men, but very big plans. Somehow they managed to infiltrate the security barrier we had around the congressman by brainwashing Rick Varner.''

"That's a terrifying thought, Larkin. To think it actually happened—''

"It did happen, Blossom," he interrupted bluntly. "There was a trial and Rick was put away for the rest of his life. But because I was the star witness, the Liberators threatened to kill me in retaliation. The California authorities were forced to place me in a Witness Security Program for my own safety. Until the Liberators are caught. Which could be soon or never.''

For long moments Blossom sat quietly as she tried to put everything he'd told her into context. All along she'd suspected that Larkin was a man undercover. At first she'd thought he might be a criminal. After all, he'd taken her out of the city against her will. But later, once she'd started learning more about him, she'd ruled out the possibility of him being on the wrong side of the law. He'd exhibited too much conscience and concern for her safety to be a bad guy. Still, she'd never expected anything like this. The man had been through hell, and from the sound of things, he was still there.

"So you're telling me those men who were firing assault rifles at us were the Liberators?"

Luke nodded. "I have no doubts about it. Somehow they were able to track me to Austin. And when they tried for a hit, you just happened to be in the way."

"But the paper—they're saying the bullets were meant for Megan and Chase," she argued. "Couldn't it be that those gunmen weren't the Liberators, but someone else after the Maitlands? Maybe it's the same person or persons who've been causing all the damage at the clinic?"

Ever since the shooting had occurred, Luke had been trying to put all the pieces of the incident together, and he'd come up with the sickening conclusion that the Liberators had discovered that Megan and her family were also his family. Killing him or any Maitland would be a trophy for the fugitives. He had to stop them before that happened, before he caused anyone in his family to be harmed. In a way, Blossom's assumptions were partly correct. The bullets had been meant for anyone who was near him, including her.

"In my opinion, the so-called accidents at the

clinic were done by someone out to cause mischief, not murder. The Liberators are a different breed. They want me dead, Blossom. And now that the damn newspaper has linked us as missing together, I can't guarantee they won't come after you, too. That's why I've got to put an end to all of this once and for all. One way or the other, I can't keep living in limbo.''

Trying not to linger on that chilling idea, Blossom asked, ''If all of this happened to you on the West Coast, what brought you to Austin?''

Shrugging, he glanced away from her. Telling her this much of the truth had been a release and he desperately wished he didn't have to lie about the rest. But now wasn't the time to reveal his true identity. He wasn't sure if there would ever be a time. The smartest thing he could do now would be to get the Liberators behind bars, then get the hell out of Austin. His aunt Megan or his siblings didn't need him. And Blossom, especially, didn't need him hanging around, ruining her bright future.

''Since Rick Varner's trial, I've been all over the place,'' he said. ''Austin just happened to be one more city where I was trying to lie low and work undetected by the Liberators. Obviously they've caught up to me.''

Blossom shook her head in wonder. ''This is like something out of a movie. I thought I'd reported on some pretty wild stories, but this one is—''

''Too bad to be believed,'' he finished for her.

Suddenly Blossom's thoughts were moving from his past and on toward tomorrow. With renewed determination, she reached for his hand and drew it up to her cheek. ''You can't go back to Austin to face those killers, Larkin. You'd be committing suicide.''

He let out a rough sigh. "I can't keep living in the shadows, either, Blossom. As far as I'm concerned it's come down to them or me."

Her eyes dark with fear, she pressed his hand against her lips. The gesture was so intimately tender, so unlike anything he'd ever received. Not only did it send a dull flush of heat creeping up his neck, it also shot a reminder to his brain as to why he'd told her all about the Liberators in the first place.

"Blossom, surely you can understand why—" He paused, then with a rueful shake of his head, tried again. "You're young and beautiful and smart."

Smiling, she wriggled closer and touched his face with her fingertips. "I don't think of myself in those terms, but I'm very glad you do."

Catching her roaming hand, he pressed it between the two of his and tried his best to ignore the heat of her body seeping into his, the round softness of her breast pushing into his upper arm.

"I'm a man who has no future," he persisted. "You, on the other hand, have a bright one ahead of you. That should be enough to tell you—anything between us would never work."

"I refuse to believe that, Larkin. You do have a future and it's with me."

A low groan slipped past his lips. "I'm seven years older than you, Blossom. I grew up on the tough side of town. I'm not a family man. I wouldn't know how to be."

"Seven years is not a lifetime," she reasoned. "And as for growing up on the tough side of town, I wasn't exactly raised in middle-class comfort. I know all about living in roach traps and having parents who neglected their duties." She frowned as a hard resolution filled her eyes. "In fact, I would have to admit that my parents are the main reason I became Blossom the Barracuda."

Forgetting that he'd captured her hand to keep its tempting search at bay, he unconsciously rubbed his fingertips over the smooth back. "You're going to have to explain that to me," he told her.

Her eyes dropped to their twined hands.

There were times when I was growing up that my mother and I were evicted from apartments. Other times we had very little to eat, or no utilities. Daddy was hardly ever around to help. Half the time he lived out of a suitcase anyway. That's why by the time I was a teenager I promised myself I would do better. I would have the security of a good job and regular paycheck."

"And you saw that in *Tattle Today TV*," he concluded.

She nodded soberly. "They offered me a good salary and a position that would allow me to get my foot into the door of broadcasting. At the time I was very young. Too young to expect more and too naive to understand the job would be—well, it would force me to report stories I didn't regard as worthy. But I needed that security, Larkin. I needed to know that tomorrow or the next day I wasn't going to be homeless or hungry. Does that make any sense to you?"

Surprisingly, it made a lot of sense to Luke. For years, he'd watched his mother and siblings live on the barest of necessities. Like Blossom, he'd never known if tomorrow would mean packing up and moving, eating three square meals or none. Living under those conditions made survival the most important thing. Ultimately, it had ruled every choice he'd made in life.

Blossom's gaze suddenly lifted to his and he felt his heart turn over as he realized he was seeing so many of his own feelings reflected in her beautiful blue eyes.

"Yes, it makes sense," he said somberly. "And I'll admit that from all you've told me, you weren't born with a silver spoon in your mouth. Which makes it even more important that you have someone better than me in your life, Blossom. I have to live my life looking over my shoulder. That can't—"

Blossom cut in, arguing, "If the Liberators are put behind bars you wouldn't have to live that way."

"There're no guarantees that will happen. Besides, the Liberators are only a part of the problem. My resolve to remain single is the biggest," he said. Then, pulling away from her, he stood and crossed over to the kitchen. At the sink he began to fill the coffeepot with water.

"Isn't it rather late to be ingesting caffeine?" she asked, abruptly changing the subject.

"I don't plan on doing much sleeping tonight," he answered.

She walked over to stand beside him. As she watched him spoon coffee grounds into the water, she said, "I guess it would be foolish of me to think I'll be the reason for your lack of sleep?"

In spite of himself, he grinned. The sight of his white teeth against his swarthy face had a wilting effect on Blossom's knees. Leaning most of her weight against the makeshift counter, she tried not to think of how it might be if he carried her into the tiny bedroom and lavished her with his own brand of attention.

"Very," he answered. "I have lots of plans to make."

And already Blossom knew she wasn't going to like any of them. "When are you going back to Austin?"

"As soon as it gets daylight," he answered.

It was all she could do to keep from shivering. "You are taking me this time. Aren't you?"

He cocked one black eyebrow in her direction. "Don't even think it."

Her mouth parted, but somehow she managed to keep from shouting at him. The cogs in her head were already turning toward tomorrow. She couldn't let Larkin go up against the Liberators alone, but for right now she knew he would refuse any sort of help she might offer. No, she thought, she had to play this all low-key. She had to make him believe she would docilely remain behind in the cabin.

"What? No argument?" he asked in disbelief.

Shrugging, she had to look away from him. Lying was not her forte and she suspected Larkin was adept at seeing through people. She didn't want to give him the chance.

"Well, naturally I want to go," she said, deliberately putting a teeny bit of a pout in her voice. "But I'd have to fight with you to do it. And I'm not totally stupid. I realize the situation might get dangerous and I'd only be one more thing for you to worry about. If you do manage to lure the Liberators to you, you'll need to be sharply focused and I might be a distraction."

His long breath slipped past the side of her cheek.

She dared to glance back at him and was relieved to see a look of appreciation on his face.

"Now you're using good sense," he praised.

Blossom smiled at him, although she did her best not to make it too sweet or meek and alert his suspicion. "Well, my job has taught me that some situations need to be handled with different tactics," she said, then glanced questioningly toward the coffeepot. "Is the coffee ready? I think I'll have a cup with you."

As if on cue, steam began to stream from the spout. Larkin turned off the fire.

"You get the cups," he said. "I'll pour in a little cold water to settle the grounds."

Moments later the cups were filled and Larkin carried his over to the couch. Blossom waited until he was settled before she sank down beside him.

He looked pointedly at her thigh and shoulder pressed up against his. "Aren't you a little close?"

Smiling, she wrinkled her nose at him. "Don't fuss at me, Larkin. I'm being agreeable about tomorrow, so let me just sit here next to you like this."

He cast her a wry glance. "Why would you want to?"

With a careful hold on her coffee mug, she somehow managed to snuggle even closer. If it hadn't been for the arm of the couch preventing his movement, he would have put several inches between them. But she had him trapped. In more ways than one, Luke decided.

"Because I like being close to you," she admitted, her voice dropping to a husky level.

He liked being close to her. Liked it all too much, he thought. And suddenly it dawned on him that surviving tomorrow would be difficult, maybe even impossible. But walking out of Blossom Woodward's life would be the hardest thing he'd ever had to do.

"Tell me what you're really like," she softly urged.

Luke closed his eyes and for long moments allowed her voice and warmth, the sweet, feminine scent of her hair and skin to fill his head and stamp his memory. "What do you mean?" he asked.

"Well, obviously you can't live the way you did before you went into the Witness Security Program. You must have had to leave all your friends and family behind."

"I didn't have any choice," he said starkly. "My being near them would only have put them in danger."

Just as it was doing now, he thought sickly. When he'd first discovered Rafe and Laura were in Austin, he'd longed to get in touch with them. The three of them had not seen one another or even been in the same city since their parents' funeral in Las Vegas. He wanted to know what had been happening in their lives and how they'd reacted to hearing that their sister Janelle had turned criminal. But instead of seeing his siblings, he'd had to keep himself disguised and hidden from anyone who might recognize him. He was just as much a prisoner as Janelle, he thought dismally.

"Do you have siblings somewhere?"

He paused as once again Rafe and Laura slipped into his mind's eye. Now there were also R.J. and Anna to consider in this whole thing. If Luke were to confide in Blossom, what kind of heyday would she have spreading the news that she'd found their black sheep brother? he wondered.

I would never betray someone I was close to in such a way.

Her promise filtered into his thoughts, yet he wasn't quite sure he could trust her. He wasn't sure he could ever trust anybody again.

"Yes. Two sisters and a brother. I'm the oldest of the bunch. But like I said, I don't—I can't see them."

"Are any of them married?"

"It's possible. Since I can't contact them, it's hard to say."

Blossom was beginning to get the picture of just how isolated Larkin was and she ached to make things different for him.

"Did you—have a special woman in your life?"

"No."

"Why?"

He swallowed a sip of coffee in hopes it would ease the ball of emotion in his throat. "Because I never knew any of them long enough to let them become special."

"And that's the way you wanted things?" she persisted.

He swallowed more of the coffee, but he still felt cold inside.

"Like I told you, Blossom. I don't have the makings of a family man. If a man gets to seeing a woman more than twice, she gets all possessive on him. I'm smart enough not to let that happen."

She sipped from her mug while carefully studying his profile. Even though the glow of the oil lamp softened his features, she sensed a hardness about him that said, even before he'd gone incognito, he'd not let himself be close to anyone. The idea saddened her greatly.

"What made you decide that you never wanted to marry? Your father?"

Everything in Luke jerked to sudden attention. Was she somehow putting things together? he wondered. Was she beginning to suspect that he was Robert Maitland's missing son?"

"What makes you ask that?"

She grimaced. "Just a hunch. You said the man neglected you," she said ruefully. "That has to mean he couldn't have been a very good husband, either. Am I right?"

Luke snorted. "He wasn't a husband. He just went through the motions of coming home once in a while and throwing his weight around as if he were the big bull in charge. He didn't know how to control himself, much less a wife and four children. Gambling and women—those were his only interests. And as far as I could tell, he wasn't even good at those two things. He ultimately lost every bit of money and every woman he tried to hold on to." He cut her a sidelong glance that was full of disgust. "So you see, I didn't exactly have good genes or a good example to follow. And when you've grown up ignorant of certain things, it's wise to avoid them. Marriage is something I plan to avoid."

"Hmm. Well, my parents' marriage wasn't exactly modeled after the Nelsons'. But I don't intend to let that stop me. I just plan on being a lot smarter than they were about choosing a spouse."

Luke wanted to tell her to forget about love and kids and all that happily-ever-after stuff. In real life it rarely happened and she'd be risking a damn lot to try it. But he didn't want to be the one to turn her cynical, to ruin her outlook on life the way his had been ruined.

"I hope you are," he murmured.

Sensing his preoccupation, Blossom placed her mug on the floor to one side, then drew her feet up under her so that she was facing him.

"Has it been a long time since you've seen your parents?"

For two years Luke had tried to forget the last time he'd seen his parents. The Las Vegas police had found their bullet-riddled bodies in a casino parking lot. Luke and the authorities suspected that the murders were gambling-related. No doubt Robert had owed thousands to disreputable loan sharks.

"Two years ago. At their funerals."

Blossom gasped at his unexpected answer. "You mean—your parents are dead?"

"They were killed—shot by someone. The police believe—well, they don't know who did it." He swallowed as his expression turned hard. "What I can't understand is why my mother was with my father. They'd been divorced for a long time and she knew he was bad news. There's no doubt in my mind that he was the target. She just happened to be around and in the way when it happened."

Blossom would have liked to ask him more, but she could see how much it was bothering him to talk about the whole incident. Two separate shootings had altered his life in a horrific way. And now someone wanted to do the same to him. It was no wonder he didn't allow himself to think about the future.

"I'm sorry, Larkin. Really sorry."

He drew in a deep breath then let it out. "Yeah. So am I."

Deciding it was best to move on, she said, "You haven't told me what you're really planning to do tomorrow."

He looked at her, his brows arched. "You think I'd actually tell you?"

A brief smile flickered on her face. "Why not? I won't be there to cause any sort of intervention."

As she waited for him to answer, she tilted her head to one side. Luke's gaze was drawn to the long blond hair falling over her shoulder and caressing one breast. In the muted glow of the oil lamp, it resembled shimmering gold threads of silk and satin.

Reaching out, he stroked his fingertips over the soft strands. "I'm not really going to *do* anything, Blossom. I'm just going to let myself be seen, then wait and see what happens."

"Where? The clinic?"

"No! I can't go back there. I'd be risking lives."

Fear squeezed her heart as a picture began to form in her mind. If it came down to a shootout, Larkin would make sure he and he alone would be the only target. "You mean other than your own?"

He nodded. "Anyway, the most likely place they'll look is my house. And since it sits alone at one end of an isolated street, I won't be endangering anyone else."

Her mind whirled. She'd already memorized the license plate number on his truck, now she needed to absorb every little scrap of information he was giving her to put with it.

"Oh, you've surprised me. I took you for an apartment kind of guy. No upkeep. No strings attached. A leave-in-a-hurry-if-need-be kind of place. A house signifies family. Are you sure you aren't lying to me?''

His eyes narrowed as they scanned her face. ''About the house or about me not being a family man?'' he wanted to know.

''Both, I think?''

''I'm not lying about either,'' he answered, then with a ragged sigh, he pulled his hand away and started to rise to his feet.

Blossom immediately caught his hand, preventing him from leaving his place beside her.

He cocked a questioning brow at her.

She swallowed as a rush of tender emotions swamped her, causing a painful breath to catch in her throat and tears to sting the back of her eyes. ''Promise me, Larkin, that tomorrow—you won't do anything foolish.''

He could actually feel her fear for him. It radiated from her like a palpable thing, and for the second time today he was overwhelmed by her concern.

''Oh, Blossom,'' he gently murmured, ''I want you to quit all this worrying. No matter what happens to me tomorrow, someone will be back here to get you. I'll make sure of that. And your life is going to go on as usual.''

No, he was wrong about that, Blossom thought with sudden resolution. Now that she'd fallen in love with him, her life was never going to be the same.

Chapter Eight

An hour before dawn something caused Blossom to jerk awake. Her heart hammered in her chest as she focused on the dim outline of the window to her right, then the chest near the foot of the narrow bed.

She'd been dreaming, she realized with a rush of relief. The exploding guns and men with green-and-brown camouflage painted on their faces had been nothing more than a nightmare.

The dream had been terrifying, but so was the idea that she'd been asleep.

For hours throughout the night, she'd lain very quiet, refusing to close her eyes as she listened for a creak from the couch or a floorboard, or for any sound to alert her that Larkin was leaving the cabin.

At some point during her vigil, exhaustion must have overtaken her and she'd fallen asleep. Dear Lord, don't let him already be gone, she prayed.

Oh, so carefully, she eased up from the lumpy mattress. Through the slit of space between the curtain and the doorjamb, she could see that the lamp was still glowing as it had been before she'd dropped off to sleep.

Maybe he'd left the lamp burning to fool her, she pondered. Maybe he was already gone.

The thought made her heart throb even faster and she could feel sweat oozing from every pore of her body. She pressed a hand between her breasts while willing her adrenaline to slow. Now wasn't the time to become hysterical, she told herself. She had to think clearly. She couldn't afford the luxury of sitting here on the bed and letting herself fall apart.

During the night, she'd been planning and scheming and she'd come to the conclusion that her only way to get back into Austin and help Larkin would be to stow away in his truck and hope he didn't find her until he was too far into the city to do anything about it.

Like a thief terrified of being caught, she tiptoed to the window she'd deliberately left raised when she'd gone to bed. Now she quietly pushed out the screen, then lifted one leg through the open space. The moment her bare toes touched the ground below, she realized she'd forgotten to put on her high heels, but the matter of shoes was hardly enough to deter her. Balancing on the foot outside, she ducked her head and pulled the rest of her body through the small opening.

Dawn was still several minutes away. She glanced around at the darkness, hoping it would conceal her movements as she crept toward the back of the little house. A trip to the bathroom was a must before she hid in the truck.

During the night the temperature had dipped to

somewhere in the upper forties. The thin T-shirt she was wearing would be little protection against the cold. Especially traveling in the back of a speeding truck. Even now she was having to clamp her teeth together to keep them from chattering.

Moments later, with her business in the bathroom finished, she moved stealthily around to the front of the house. Pausing at the corner, she was relieved to see Larkin's truck still parked in the same spot. He was nowhere in sight, and from the looks of the heavy dew covering the windshield, he'd not yet been in the truck this morning. That meant he was still in the house and she had little time to waste.

Like a rabbit with a fox on its tail, she scampered across the rough ground, climbed up the truck's back bumper, then over into the bed.

Unfortunately, she found the large space empty with nothing to hide behind or under. Her only choice was to spread herself flat against the cold metal floor and pray that Larkin didn't bother glancing in the back before he climbed into the cab.

She wasn't sure how long she lay there waiting when she finally heard the front door softly creak open, then bang shut. From the stiffness of her cold body, it felt like hours, but faint streaks of pink light in the sky overhead told her it could have only been minutes.

In a matter of seconds Larkin's boots were crunching over the rough ground. Blossom held her breath and willed her shivering limbs to remain motionless.

Finally, the footsteps sounded as though they were on top of her. Facedown, she kept her eyes closed, her body rigid as she waited for the clicking release of the door handle. Once he was inside and driving, she would be safe until daylight. And by then, they should be in Austin, she thought with a sense of triumph.

"What the hell—"

The explosion of words ripped through Blossom's cold body and shot her to her feet. She could see the faint outline of his body standing beside the truck and she didn't need a light to tell her his face was rigid with anger.

"There's no way I'm going to let you go to Austin alone," she said in a rush. "So there's no use trying to make me stay here."

He uttered a curse. "Last night you agreed that you should stay here. I was a fool to trust you!"

One hand lunged for her. She jumped back.

"Larkin, I didn't lie!" she burst out while inching backward and away from him. "I did agree that I should stay here, but I didn't actually tell you I would. You assumed that on your own."

"Well, you can bet your sweet little behind that's the last thing I'm going to assume about you!"

Vaulting into the back of the truck, he grabbed for her. With a loud yelp, Blossom managed to jump out of his reach, but she was not nearly quick enough to make it over the tailgate. He caught her around the waist and hauled her up against him.

The solid warmth of his body was too wonderful to resist. Like a flash, she twisted so that she was facing him and flung her arms around his neck. "Larkin! Let me go with you," she pleaded. "I can help. You need me. You know that you do."

Luke silently groaned. Blossom was right. He did need her, but not in the way she thought. Not to help him wage a battle against the Liberators. That was a man's job, and the way he needed Blossom had everything to do with her being a woman.

"I won't let you go. Nothing you can say or do will change my mind," he said flatly. "Not even feminine persuasion."

His expression was hidden from her in the gray morning light. "Is that what you think I'm doing now? If I remember correctly, you grabbed me. Not the other way around."

Precious moments were slipping by. Luke should have already been on his way to Austin. Yet the feel of Blossom in his arms made him linger and yearn for things to be different.

"I didn't ask you to put your arms around me," he pointed out in a husky voice.

"You didn't ask me to do this, either," she murmured softly. "But I'm going to, anyway."

Luke didn't have a chance to question or wonder. Suddenly she was kissing him again. Just as she had yesterday morning with that same warm and giving urgency that knocked the earth right out from under his feet.

Instinctively, his hands splayed intimately against her back and drew her more tightly against him. His tongue slipped between her teeth, and through a hazy fog of desire he heard her soft moan of acceptance, felt her fingers press deeper into the back of his neck.

This was all he would ever have of her, he thought bleakly. This moment, this kiss would have to last him a lifetime. Once he left this cabin, he could never see her again. And even if he did, it could never be like this.

The knowledge made him even more reluctant to

end the embrace, but he finally found the strength to lift his head and ease her away from him.

"Get in the cabin, Blossom," he ordered hoarsely.

"No, Larkin. I'm not about to let you face those killers alone! Don't you understand that I care about you?"

Pain tightened around his heart. "You care about a story, Blossom. That's all you care about."

She gasped. "That's a cheap shot, Larkin!"

Yes, it was, he thought sickly. But it was easier to let himself believe she was that barracuda the public knew rather than the warm, giving woman in his arms.

"Maybe so," he agreed. "But no one ever accused me of being nice. Better you know that now than later."

"Larkin—"

He didn't give her a chance to say more. With a hand on her wrist, he hauled her over the tailgate and onto the porch.

"What are you doing?" she cried as he grabbed one of the straight-backed wooden chairs and pulled it and her into the house.

"Making sure you stay put," he answered. "At least until I get gone."

Still gripping her wrist with one hand, he rummaged through a wooden box sitting in one corner of the kitchen floor. When he pulled out a piece of braided grass rope, Blossom knew his intentions.

"No, Larkin! No! Don't tie me up, please! You can't—I won't give you any more trouble. Just let me—"

"Don't bother with your promises," he interrupted.

He plopped her down on the hard wooden seat and she stared up at him in horror.

"This is outrageous," she wailed. "I'll never forgive you for this! Or for throwing my phone out the window!"

He began to bind her to the back of the chair with the scratchy rope. "I'm sorry you forced me into this, Blossom. Maybe this will make you realize that headstrong attitude of yours is only going to get you into trouble. But in the meantime, I'm going to make sure you don't cause me any more than you already have."

Luke tied the rope behind the chair back, careful to make sure the knot was loose enough so that she could free herself after the few minutes it took him to drive away.

Satisfied that the rope would hold her for now, he walked around to the front of the chair and looked down at her mutinous face. Her cheeks were red, and between tangled strands of blond hair, her eyes were spitting fire. Luke realized with a bit of self-disgust that he was more than tempted to kiss her again.

"Remember what I told you yesterday. Make sure no one catches you here in the cabin, unless it's a lawman or a person you know. I'll send someone back for you as soon as I can."

Suddenly the anger in her eyes was replaced with outright horror. "Aren't you coming back for me?"

"No."

"Why?"

He heaved out a heavy breath. "Our time together is over, Blossom. The next thing you'll hear about me is that I'm gone."

The urge to scream at him parted her lips, but she

clamped back the sound. Any argument, screams or sobs she gave him now would fall on deaf ears.

"Or dead?" she asked quietly.

Something like regret flickered over his face, then he turned and walked out the door.

Five minutes later, Blossom managed to loosen the rope enough to allow her hands to reach around the back of the chair. After a few feeble tugs on the knot, it jerked free.

"The damn man," she muttered as she jumped to her feet, "he doesn't even know how to keep a woman tied up! How does he expect to fend off a band of killers?"

As soon as she spoke the words aloud, she realized Larkin had purposely left the rope loose enough to allow her to escape a few minutes after he left.

Larkin didn't want to place her in any sort of danger here or back in Austin. That could only mean he cared. But none of that would matter if something happened to him, Blossom thought with wild despair.

Rushing to the tiny bedroom, she rifled through the chest until she found a long-sleeved shirt to wear as a jacket. Her feet, however, were another thing. She couldn't walk out of this wilderness in high heels. Yet she seriously doubted that her bare feet could make the trek.

Think, Blossom. All you need to do is get rid of the heels.

The inner voice had her grabbing up the beige high heels and whacking them against the corner bedpost until both heels fell off. The result was a pair of lumpy flats that she hoped would hold together until she reached the main highway.

Outside, it was beginning to grow light. No doubt Larkin was already miles away. The idea shook her, but she refused to give up. She had no doubt that once she got to Austin she could find him and help. Whether she would arrive in time was the crucial question. But no one, not even Larkin, knew how long it would take for the Liberators to rise to his bait. If luck was riding with her, she could reach him before that happened.

Two solid hours of walking passed before Blossom came to an intersection of dirt road. She was wiping her sweaty face with the back of her sleeve while trying to decide which direction to take when a pickup truck pulled to a halt beside her. On the side of the door was written in large block letters, Texas State Game and Wildlife Biology. Behind the wheel an older man looked at her with concern.

"Are you lost, miss?"

Relieved, Blossom hurried over to the truck and spoke to him through the open window. "I—uh, my boyfriend and I were camping and we had a little argument," she said with crossed fingers behind her back. "He took off with the vehicle and left me to walk."

He chuckled. "Sounds like you need to get a new boyfriend."

"I aim to do that as soon as I get back to Austin," she agreed with a weary smile. "Is there any way you could give me a lift to the main highway?"

Leaning across the bench seat, the driver opened the passenger door and motioned for Blossom to climb in. "I can do better than that. I just happen to be going to Austin."

Blossom hopped into the truck and quickly sent a silent thank-you toward heaven.

At eleven that morning a taxi let her out in front of her apartment. To her surprise, yellow crime-scene tape had been placed across the door and the jambs. But then she suddenly remembered she was missing and presumed to be kidnapped. The police had probably searched her apartment for clues to her whereabouts. As soon as her return was detected, she would become breaking news.

Ignoring the tape, she stuck her key in the lock and hurried inside. Five minutes later she was out of the shower and gobbling down two pieces of bologna jammed between a slice of sourdough bread. Between bites she reached for the phone and punched in a number.

Her call was picked up on the second ring. She was relieved to hear J.P.'s voice on the other end. If someone other than the fatherly police officer in Investigations had answered, she would have pretended to be someone else.

"J.P., it's Blossom. Can you talk without anyone hearing you?"

"Blossom! Where the hell are you?" he barked in a low voice.

She smiled as she pictured the look of surprise on his droopy, hound-dog face. "At my apartment. But not for long," she answered. "I need some information. Pronto."

"So do a hell of a lot of detectives who are working the Maitland shooting. They all think you're kidnapped or dead."

"I'm neither, and please don't give my where-

abouts away just yet, J.P. I don't want anyone, press
or law officials, swarming over my apartment.''

The older man snorted. ''That's a good one coming
from you.''

Where Blossom's job was concerned, J.P. had
never been bashful about voicing his disapproval. Before, she'd always let his remarks roll off her back.
But for some reason this time she could hear Larkin's
voice echoing in J.P.'s words. Maybe it was time to
let everyone know she'd been working hard so that
she could move on to a more meaningful job.

''I understand I'm the last person who should be
asking for privacy, but I have a good reason, J.P.''

''What—''

''I don't have time to explain now,'' she said, cutting in. ''But it could mean life or death.''

''Cut the dramatics, Blossom. I'm not your audience.''

So now she was the little boy who'd cried wolf one
too many times, she thought dismally. ''This is for
real!'' she practically yelled. ''This has nothing to do
with my program.''

''I've never known you to do anything that didn't
have to do with your program.''

Three days ago she would have laughed at J.P.'s
reply. Today it took her aback. She'd never thought
of her life as being so driven by her work. But her
time with Larkin had taken her away from the cameras and microphones and relentless digging for one
more scoop. For the past two days her mind had been
consumed with the man who'd saved her life. At this
moment, she realized that getting another story meant
nothing. Keeping Larkin safe and near was all that
mattered to her.

Dear Lord, she was totally, desperately in love with the man! How had that happened? She'd only known the man for two days! But so much had passed between them in that small amount of time. Enough to tell her heart that he was the man she wanted to spend the rest of her life with.

"Blossom! Are you still there? What the heck is going on?"

The officer's voice jolted her back to the moment. Gripping the phone, she reached for a pad and pen. "I'm here, J.P. I'm here. I need you to run a license plate number for me."

Amid some grumbling, she gave him the number and he left the phone long enough to put a search through the computer. She was tapping her toe and the pen by the time he came back on the line.

"The name is Michael Larkin. You want the address?"

"Yes! Yes! Hurry!"

"Just a minute, now," he began in a tone that Blossom recognized as the one he used preceding a lecture. "Maybe you'd better tell me who this guy is first. I'm not going to—"

Blossom groaned. "I told you, J.P., this isn't about my show or—"

"You have an interest in this man for some reason. What is it?"

She loved him wildly. That was her interest, she thought. Aloud, she said, "He might be in danger. I want to help him."

"What kind of danger? You'd better let the police handle it."

Fear shot through her. She'd promised Larkin she

wouldn't blow his cover. He might not believe her, but she'd die before she broke that promise.

"No! I can't do that, J.P. Please, just give me the address. If I see that the man needs help from the police, I'll call. Promise."

J.P. uttered a few more grumbles before he finally gave in and read the address back to Blossom. As she scratched it down on the notepad, she breathed a great sigh of relief.

"You're a peach, J.P. I owe you big time for this."

"Damn right. Longhorn tickets might do it. Fifty-yard line."

"You got 'em," she said with a laugh, then dropped the phone back on its hook.

In her bedroom she raced from the closet to the chest of drawers and threw on underwear, jeans and a thin black sweater with quarter-length sleeves and a boat neck. All the while, her mind was clicking through information like a computer chip.

She had Larkin's address, the place where he was going to try to lure the Liberators. What could she do from this point? she asked herself. If she alerted the police, they would no doubt blow his whole plan. He would never forgive her.

Groaning with frustration, she picked up a wide-tooth comb and began to yank it through her freshly shampooed hair. Face it, Blossom, your information about the man is as scarce as hen's teeth. You don't even know his real name.

Tossing down the comb, she went back out to the living room and grabbed up the pad and pencil with Larkin's address. Below it she began to write down all the clues she had so far about the man.

Twenty-eight. A security agent in California.

Forced into Witness Security. The oldest of four siblings. One brother, two sisters. Parents divorced. Father had been addicted to women and gambling. Both shot and killed together.

The short but tragic facts buzzed in her brain. Why did some of this sound so familiar? she asked herself. There were parts of this puzzle that were similar to something she'd been working on. But what?

Past stories and information once again began to click with blurring speed through her mind, and all the while three things kept popping to the forefront. Four siblings. Two boys, two girls. Parents shot and killed.

After a few moments, her eyes grew wide with wonder and she hurried over to her personal computer. Once it was up and running, she quickly pulled up the file she'd kept since the Maitland story had broken a year ago. After a few seconds of scanning her notes, everything settled into place.

Larkin was Luke Maitland!

For a few moments she was so stunned all she could do was stare blankly at the wall. Why had she not guessed before now? The clues had been there for her to see.

You were too busy falling in love with the man to see anything else, Blossom.

She pressed her palms to her hot cheeks. What must he be thinking? She'd been so quick to point out to him that she was a good reporter! He must have been silently laughing himself silly. She'd been right under the nose—no, make that right in the arms—of the man she'd been diligently searching during the past two months and had never guessed!

Oh, why hadn't he told her? The answer to that

made her groan with shame. In his eyes, she was
Blossom the Barracuda and Luke Maitland was to be
her super scoop. He'd felt he couldn't trust her. He
believed she would place her job at *Tattle Today TV*
over him. Especially once she'd learned he was the
long-lost sibling of Rafe, Laura, R.J. and Anna. But
he was wrong, she thought desperately. So wrong.

Yes, she'd been driven to succeed at her job on
Tattle Today TV, she had to admit. Since she'd begun
as a fledging reporter, she'd thrown herself into the
role. She was relentless when necessary, even bad-
gering when it came to acquiring information she
needed. But that was only because she'd been determined to do her very best, to be everything her irresponsible parents had never been. Maybe somewhere
along the way she had gone overboard. Yet in her
heart, her intentions had always been sincere. She'd
never meant to hurt anyone. Would she ever be able
to make Luke understand that?

Forget understanding, Blossom, she silently yelled
at herself. Right now you've got to make sure he sur-
vives this crazy scheme to flush out the Liberators!

Jumping to her feet, she began to pace around the
living room of her small apartment. It was closing in
on noon. Her producer was too cheap to go out for
lunch. Right about now he was eating from a brown
bag in his office. She could call him, but the instant
he heard her voice, her face would be plastered on
every television screen from San Antonio to Waco
and parts beyond.

Her disappearance had been linked to Luke and no
doubt he would also be connected to her return. If the
Liberators had been smart enough to track Luke to
Texas, they had enough sense to watch the news.

Once it was broadcast that she'd reappeared in Austin, they would suspect Luke was back in town and go after him.

That is what the man wants, Blossom. Yes, but so did the police, she argued with herself. The key was to make them all come together at once. Before anyone got hurt. But was she a good enough reporter to make that happen? If she wasn't, the man she loved might very well die. And even if he didn't, he might end up hating her for the rest of their lives. But she had no choice that she could see. No choice at all.

Her hands trembling, she went to the phone and punched in the number for a taxi.

Chapter Nine

From his hidden nook in the kitchen, Luke heard the gunmen's footsteps long before they entered the long, dark room. Two sets of feet moving purposely toward him. There would be three more somewhere in the house, the yard or a waiting vehicle. These two would have to be used for leverage to capture the others.

His mouth dry, his heart pounding, he waited. And waited. All the while thoughts of Blossom filled his head. Thank God she was far away from here, far away from this deadly game he was playing. He wanted her safe and happy. More than anything he wanted for himself.

From the corner of his eye, he could see the toe of a boot appear less than ten inches away. One more step past the wall he was hiding behind and the men would be exposed to his gun.

Not daring to breathe, he stepped out of his hiding place. "Hold it!" he ordered roughly. "And drop your weapons."

"Wait a minute, buddy—we're not who you think we are," one of the men quickly blurted out.

"We're with Austin SWAT," his companion added in a rush.

"Yeah, sure. Austin SWAT doesn't know anything about this—"

"Better look out the front, Mr. Maitland. Your yard is swarming with law officials by now."

The "Mr. Larkin" caught his attention. Even if the Liberators knew his undercover name, he doubted they would use it at this point in the game.

Ripping a flashlight from his pocket, he aimed the circle of light at the two men and was instantly shocked to see the police officers standing in front of him.

From a walkie-talkie anchored to the shoulder of the officer closest to him, a voice said, "Jones! Rodriguez! Have you found him yet? Is he okay?"

The men looked at Luke for an answer. Dazed by this sudden turn of events, he gave them an affirmative nod, then handed over his weapon.

Outside on the lawn several patrol cars were jammed together at odd angles. Their flashing lights bounced off the front of the house and illuminated the nearby street. Policemen were swarming here and there while several more SWAT members were loading the last of the handcuffed Liberators into a van.

Before Luke could make sense of it all, one of the officers shuffled him to a patrol car and introduced him to the captain in charge of operations.

"We're happy to find you safe, Mr. Maitland," he said as he pumped Luke's hand, "and I'm sure you're going to be happy to hear your long ordeal is over."

Luke stared at him in wonder. "But how—"

The older man smiled and pointed to a figure sitting in the back of the patrol car. "Miss Woodward. Why don't you let her explain it to you while we head down to the station. I'm going to need you to identify these guys, and I have to get your statement," he said.

The captain quickly climbed into the car. Someone opened the back passenger door for Luke. He had no choice but to slide inside beside Blossom, who immediately flung herself at him and clamped her arms around his neck.

"Oh, Luke! I've been so scared. But now you're safe," she whispered tearfully. "*Really* safe."

The feel of her soft, warm body pressed next to his was something he'd thought he'd never experience again. For a few precious moments it didn't matter what had happened or that she and these officers knew he was actually Luke Maitland; he allowed himself to hold her.

"You know who I am," he said after he finally managed to set her away from him.

Smiling tenderly, she cupped her hands around his face as though it was the most precious thing she'd ever laid eyes on. A kiss could not have touched him more and he cast an embarrassed glance at the captain in the front seat to see if he was witnessing their exchange, but to his relief, the other man's eyes were safely on the traffic.

"Once I got back to Austin this morning, I figured it out."

He grimaced. "I didn't plan on you getting back so soon."

She laughed softly and the sound warmed him, amazed him that such a little thing could affect him so.

"That's because you underestimate me," she said.

"It's a good thing she did, Mr. Maitland. Otherwise—well, those men were closing in on you fast. They were at your back door when we arrived. Thanks to Miss Woodward's quick alert, we kept them from getting into the house."

His gaze on Blossom, he shook his head ruefully. "I want to be angry with you, but right now—" He cast another quick glance at the captain, then looked at her with misgiving. "We'll talk about it later," he promised.

It seemed to Blossom that hours had passed before she and Luke were finally able to sign their statements and leave the police station. Thanks to the kindly captain, they were allowed to go out of the building a back way, far from the press that had already gathered out front.

"I never thought you'd be wanting to avoid the media," Luke said as she drove the two of them toward her apartment. "Aren't you missing being the star on the big scene with the latest breaking news?"

She winced at the mockery in his voice. During their time at the station, she'd hoped he'd realized everything she had done, she'd done for him and him alone. Apparently, he believed there had been more going on than her deal with the police to help him.

"I'll admit I deserve a little of your cynicism, Luke. But not all. I haven't given any sort of story about you to the press. Not even to my own producer."

His lips twisted with mockery. "That's why all those reporters with microphones and cameras are gathered around the station house? Come on, Blossom, I'm not Larkin like I first told you. But I'm not an idiot, either.''

She heaved out a frustrated breath. ''Those are reporters who listen in on police scanners. Apparently they smelled a story and headed to the station to try to catch a better whiff. I'll admit I'm guilty of doing the very same thing. But not tonight and not with you.''

Her last words were spoken with a bit of anger, as though he should have been trusting her all along. But it wasn't that easy for Luke. It never would be. She needed to know just what a hard, distrustful man he was before she let her hopes about the two of them go any further.

Sighing, he raked a hand through his hair. The act suddenly made him realize that he could now go get it cut to the shorter length he used to wear and let its true brown color return.

Another thought struck him and he quickly bent forward and peeled the contacts from his eyes.

''What are you doing?'' she asked.

''Getting rid of these,'' he said, holding up his palm to show her the colored contacts. ''My eyes are green, not blue. My hair is brown, not black. And my name is Luke, not Larkin.''

In spite of the roughness of his voice, she dared to smile at him. After all, he was safe and beside her. Right now that was enough for her to feel utterly blessed.

''It must feel good to know you can finally be yourself again.''

He shrugged. ''It's been so long since I've been Luke Maitland, I'm not sure I remember the man.

Maybe he's the same as Larkin except the coloring is different.''

Blossom slowly regarded him and came up with the deduction that everything was happening too quickly for him. He needed time to think and to come to grips with the fact that tonight his life had drastically changed. He was no longer Michael Larkin, a man hiding from the world and maybe even himself.

"It will all come back to you, Luke," she said softly. "You just need time."

His chiseled features tightened. "That's something I don't have. I'm sure by tomorrow my story will hit the news." He slanted an accusing look her way. "Or has it already?"

The apartment complex where she lived had come into view. Blossom eased her foot off the accelerator and braked for a stop sign. As she waited for passing traffic, she looked over at him.

"Other than Captain Morales, I haven't told anyone about you. But I'm not going to predict how long it will be before some of those officers talk. Your Witness Security cover has been blown. Which, as far as I can see, hurts nothing. You finally have the freedom to be yourself again. See your brothers and sisters and meet the family you've never known."

"I'm not sure I want to do that, Blossom."

His grim retort took her aback, but instead of pressing him for reasons, she said, "Here's my apartment. You can stay here with me tonight."

Outside in the cool fall air, Luke followed her to the door, then inside. She motioned for him to take a seat on the long couch. He looked around at the simple furnishings. The proof that Blossom was a career woman rather than Little Miss Homemaker was evident in the clutter scattered around the room.

Tossing her handbag onto a computer desk, she said, "I'll make coffee and something for us to eat. Make yourself at home."

She headed to the kitchen and he sank onto the couch, but instantly he was overcome with restlessness. Too much had happened tonight and in the past few days for him to unwind instantly from it all. Besides, now that he was completely alone with Blossom he was finding it hard to ignore his desire for her. The last thing he needed to do was sleep with a virgin who believed herself in love with him.

Back on his feet, he joined her in the small cooking-dining area. She was at the refrigerator door, bent slightly at the waist as she searched a lower shelf. The jeans she was wearing hugged her shapely rear and legs. The little black sweater molded to her small waist and full breasts, outlining their alluring shape. Each time he looked at her all he could think about was the moments at the cabin when he'd held her in his arms and she'd offered herself to him in such a trusting, giving way. For some reason he couldn't understand, she wanted him. And that in itself was a powerful aphrodisiac.

"I can't stay here tonight, Blossom," he blurted out. "If you'll take me to my house—"

She whipped around to stare at him. "Don't be crazy, Luke! That was a three-ring circus over there earlier. Reporters are probably camped out there for the night. You don't want to deal with them, do you?"

He swiped a hand over his face. "No. But—well, I'll call a taxi and go to a motel."

Blossom shut the refrigerator door and walked over to where he stood near one corner of the dining table. He looked lost and torn and exhausted. Everything inside her wanted to comfort him, love him, make him happy. But would he ever let her? she wondered sadly.

"You really want to get away from me in the worst kind of way, don't you?"

There was pain in her softly spoken question and the sound of it stabbed Luke deeply.

"Blossom, this is...I told you..." He stopped and shook his head as the right words failed to come to him. "Damn it all! Have you forgotten what I told you? There can be no *us!* No *we!*"

Her chin inched forward. "Did you ever stop to think you could be wrong about that?"

"Not wrong. Smart. I—"

She didn't allow him to go on. Instead she stepped closer and placed her palms against his hard, warm chest. "You were wrong about my helping you, Luke. The police nabbed the gunmen. You're safe and they're behind bars. Something you've been wanting for a long time. You could be wrong about us."

Feeling more cornered by the second, his frustration turned to anger. Not anger at her, but rather at himself for allowing the human emotion of wanting her to get in the way of his common sense. Now she'd somehow managed to insert herself into his life and he had to get her out. Fast. Before he did something both of them would later regret.

"I could have managed alone," he said flatly. "I wasn't dead yet!"

Flabbergasted, she stared at him. "There were five of them! One of you. If you—"

"You called the police," he blasted at her. "You promised not to reveal my identity. But I guess nothing can stop you from being Blossom the Barracuda. Not even me!"

Never had she been so crushed in her life, and though she'd learned to stem her tears long ago, they were stronger than she was this time. Before she could turn her back to him, her eyes filled with watery betrayal.

Quickly ducking her head, she stepped away from him and gulped in a deep, painful breath.

"It probably won't mean anything to you, Luke," she said in a small voice. "But I'll say it, anyway. I didn't tell the police. They discovered it through a background check. And then I had no choice but to explain your story to the captain. He agreed to keep it quiet for as long as he could."

"A dead person wouldn't have shown up on a background check," he argued. "I died when I became Larkin. Information about Luke Maitland was wiped from the slate. That's one of the reasons your attempts to track me failed."

A sudden burst of anger gave her the strength to whirl and face him once again. "And that's the way you want to stay, isn't it? Sometimes I get the feeling you really wish you were dead! So you wouldn't be tempted to need or love anyone! Maybe I should have done you a favor and let the Liberators kill you—you ungrateful lout!"

"What could you know about it? How could you know about me?" He snarled the questions.

Instantly, her expression and voice gentled. "Because we're two of a kind, Luke. We both know what it's like to be hurt, belittled, unwanted. It makes you scared to feel anything for anybody. You hide your loneliness behind a tough face while you wonder why you had to be different, why you couldn't have come from a normal home with loving and devoted parents."

The rigid lines of his face began to soften as her words echoed the lonely cries in his heart. "If you know all of this, Blossom, then you must surely understand why—" he lifted his arms, then let them fall helplessly back down to his sides "—we can't have a relationship. People like us aren't good at it."

Sensing a chip in his armor, she placed her hands upon each of his shoulders and moved so that the front of her body was brushing his. "We will be good at it, Luke," she whispered. "Because we know how precious it is to be needed and loved. We won't ever take that for granted."

If he could only believe her, Luke thought. To spend the rest of his life loving this woman would be a gift from heaven. But since when had he ever deserved gifts, he asked himself. Especially coming from that high a source.

"You make a good argument, Blossom, but—"

She leaned her forehead into his. "I'm not arguing, darling. I'm reasoning."

Groaning, he snared her waist with both hands. "You're a temptress," he murmured against her lips. "A siren with long golden hair and a body made to be loved."

Beneath his, her lips spread into a beguiling smile, and she whispered, "A body made for you, Luke. Only for you."

The promise of her words and the sweetness of her lips moving against his was enough to scatter Luke's weary senses. Anchoring her warm body tightly against his, he captured her lips with a full-blown kiss.

His loving assault sent Blossom's head reeling, and for the next few moments it was all she could do to hang on to him and let him drink his fill of her mouth.

When his head finally lifted, she was panting for air. At the same time her body burned to link with his in the most basic human way, and the need only intensified as his lips found the side of her neck.

Hungrily he nibbled his way to the juncture of her shoulder. Overcome with the sensation of his warm mouth against her skin, Blossom let her head fall limply backward, a soft whimper of delight sounding in her throat. Fueled by need and her heady response, Luke continued his downward path until the material of her sweater got in the way.

"Oh, Luke, love me," she whispered in a raw, hoarse voice. "That's all I want from you. That's all I'll ever want from you."

At this moment he wanted nothing more than to give her what they both wanted. It didn't matter who she was or who he had been.

Impatiently, he yanked on the loose neck to completely expose her shoulder and the top of one breast. She gripped his back as his tongue traced a warm moist trail to the edge of her bra.

The white lacy material forced him to pause long enough for a flash of sanity to break into the fog of desire gripping his senses. Dear Lord, she was an innocent virgin! She was saving herself for the man she was going to spend the rest of her life with. Not a man like him.

His head jerked up at the same time he set her from him. She stared at him in bewilderment, and as Luke took in her swollen red lips and disheveled hair, he groaned with a mixture of self-disgust and desire.

"Now do you see why I can't stay here, Blossom?"

Her head jerked back and forth. "This isn't wrong!"

Turning away from her, he purposely put several steps between them, then glared back over his shoulder at her. "It damn sure isn't right! A few more moments and I would have been carrying you to bed!"

Her brows lifted, then a provocative smile curled the corners of her lips. "That's exactly what I want you to do, Luke."

Muttering a curse, he threw up his hands and stared at the ceiling. "You don't know what you're saying. Or doing."

Shoving a tangle of hair from her face, she hurried over and caught his forearm. He stepped back as though she were a flame threatening to scorch him. Still, he didn't go so far as to pull loose of her fingers, and Blossom took quick advantage by sliding her hand up his arm, over his shoulder and finally settling it against his rough cheek.

"Oh, yes I do, Luke Maitland. I'm saying I love you. I want us to be together. In every way."

I love you. He'd heard those words before, but not with any meaning behind them. Not the way Blossom was saying them. The conviction in her voice terrified him. He didn't want this woman's love. He didn't want something he would ultimately have to give up.

"You think that now, Blossom. But after a few days, a few weeks, when you really got to know me, you would be asking yourself what you ever saw in me. I'm not the family man you need, Blossom."

Unconvinced, she continued to search his face with eyes that glowed with love.

Luke groaned with frustration. "Look, the last thing you need or want is a rolling stone like your father," he continued. "You more or less said that yourself."

"That's true. I always swore I would be smarter than my mother about choosing a mate. And I'll admit I had always planned to be older and wiser before I let myself fall in love. I wanted my career to be at its peak and everything neat and in its place before I made a commitment to a man. But you came along and wrecked all my well-laid plans. Now I don't care a damn about neatness—I just want you."

And what Blossom the Barracuda went after, she usually got. Since he'd been in Austin, Luke had already witnessed that firsthand. In fact, he was living proof. She'd been hunting Luke Maitland for a story and she'd found him. Now she wanted more from him. But he didn't have it to give.

Before he could change his mind and allow the tender look in her eyes to sway him, Luke turned and stalked to the door.

Instantly Blossom raced after him. "Where are you going?"

His hand on the doorknob, he paused. "I'm getting the hell out of this town. The only way I can make you see reason is to put some time and distance between us. Later, you'll thank me.''

"But what about your family? Your brothers and sisters. Aren't you going to see them before you go?"

Her question swung him around to face her. "No," he said flatly. "It appears they're all happy and doing well. They don't need me barging into their lives and messing things up."

Blossom had to struggle to keep from shouting at him. "I don't think they would consider it barging. If you—"

"I could have gotten one or all of them killed, Blossom. Megan and Chase were nearly mowed down with bullets just because they were within a few feet of me. No, my family doesn't need that."

"But your enemies are behind bars! You're not going to endanger them with a simple visit—"

He glanced over his shoulder to glare at her. "If they knew the truth about the shooting, do you honestly think they'd feel good about me coming here to Austin? I imagine in their eyes I'd be just a rung up from Janelle. Besides, they already have suspicions that Luke Maitland has been sabotaging the clinic, I don't want to have to prove my innocence to them!"

She shook her head with disbelief. "They won't blame you for the shooting or the clinic mishaps or anything that Janelle did when—"

His hand was suddenly gripping her shoulder. "If you care as much about me as you say you do, you won't tell the Maitlands about me. Not until I'm gone from here."

There was no reaching him, Blossom realized. At least not tonight. He wanted to turn his back on her

and all the Maitlands. On love and family. Something
he'd never had. If she hadn't understood that fear was
driving him, she would have been furious. As it was,
she managed to hold her emotions down to a simmering anger.

"Oh, believe me, Luke, if they hear about you, it
won't be from me! Why should I be the bearer of bad
tidings?" She swatted his hand away from her shoulder. "Now, why don't you go? It was a long walk
from Pedernales and I've just realized you weren't
worth the effort!"

A smile that had nothing to do with pleasure suddenly twisted his lips. "Now you're finally getting it,
babe. You're obviously smarter than I thought."

She stared at him for long, painful moments, then
turned and ran from the room.

His heart feeling like a chunk of lead, Luke let
himself out of the apartment, then carefully locked
the door behind him.

Chapter Ten

"**I** owe my life to Michael Larkin. This is Blossom Woodward reporting for *Tattle Today TV*. Thank you and good evening."

The camera eye went dark, cuing Blossom that she was no longer on the air. With a sigh of relief she began to unclip the microphone from the front of her dress.

She'd just spent the whole thirty-minute show giving her audience only partial truths and explanations about the days she'd been missing and the reason for her disappearance.

Damn Luke Maitland, anyway, she thought crossly. First he'd forced her to hide with him, then he'd made her fall in love with him, and now she'd stooped to lying for him. Where was it all going to end? she wondered. The answer to that was too scary to ponder.

"Great job, Blossom! The phones started ringing five minutes after you went on air. The ratings are going to skyrocket over this. You couldn't have planned it better if you'd tried!''

Blossom cast a tired glance at Billy, her producer, a man who wasn't much older than she, but who, because of his receding hairline and flabby body, looked at least ten years her senior.

''You mean I should try to get myself killed more often?'' she asked cynically.

He waved away her question. ''Of course not—we're all thrilled to have you back.'' His smile had the look of a broker who knew he'd just made thousands by sheer luck. ''You can see that the station has been flooded with calls and flowers for you. Are you sure you can't get this Larkin guy to come on the show?''

''No.'' Blossom grabbed up her notes and headed out of the broadcast room and down a narrow maze of hallways.

The producer followed quickly on her heels. ''The ratings would go through the roof—give us a lot more leverage with our sponsors. We could probably manage a raise for you.''

''I said no, Billy. Forget it.''

He groaned loudly. ''Well, surely you could get something on tape from him. It wouldn't be as good as live—with the two of you together. But it would be better than nothing.''

She entered her nook of an office and snatched her jacket from the back of a chair. ''He won't do it. Don't ask.''

''But...but, Blossom,'' Billy began to splutter, ''this is crazy! The man should be more than eager to do a little bragging in front of the camera.''

During those first hours as Luke had dragged her

to the cabin, she'd thought him to be the most arrogant, self-important man she'd ever met. But it hadn't taken her long to see that he was really just the opposite. The Luke she now knew would be the last person ever to brag about himself to anyone, much less an audience of thousands. In his eyes he wasn't nearly good enough to be anyone's hero. Especially hers, she thought bleakly.

"I realize this will come as a surprise to you, Billy, but there are actually people out there who do things out of the goodness of their hearts. Not for fame or fortune. Larkin is one of those people."

"Great! The more sincere the better. We'll play up his modesty and the public will eat it up. You can—"

He stopped as she turned a glare on him. "Good night, Billy. And don't expect me in tomorrow. I need time off."

Billy's mouth fell open. Blossom had never asked for days off. She was a workaholic putting in far more time on her job than the station required of her. This was a different woman standing before him.

"How much time?"

Blossom headed out of the office. "I haven't decided yet. I'll call you."

Across town Luke switched off the television and closed his eyes. He didn't know why he'd tuned in to Blossom's program. Maybe a part of him had believed she would blast the airways with the news that she'd found Luke Maitland, that he'd nearly gotten her killed, then taken her prisoner. No doubt the story would have been a sensation. Especially the part about him tying her to a chair, then leaving her in the wilderness, he thought grimly. It would have been very easy for her to put a dark slant on every move he'd made and place herself in the spotlight.

Instead, she'd done none of those things. She'd kept her word about not revealing his identity. She'd gone even further and painted Michael Larkin a hero for saving her life at the clinic.

With a moan of agony, he pushed himself out of the armchair and began to pace around the living room. Near the door, his bags sat packed and waiting to be loaded into the truck. All he had to do now was lock the door and drive away.

That should be easy enough, he told himself. He'd done it a hundred times before and each time he'd not looked back. He'd made himself forget everything he'd left behind. But this time would be different. He'd be leaving brothers and sisters, an aunt and cousins. His family.

Blossom had insisted they would want to see him, to include him in their loving circle. Was she right? he wondered. Or would the Maitlands and Blossom be better off if he left Austin and stayed out of their lives?

By the time Blossom managed to drive back to her apartment, she was shaking all over and tears were burning the backs of her eyes. It was true she was exhausted. The past few days had been a whirlwind both physically and emotionally. But she had to be honest with herself. Exhaustion wasn't the reason she was breaking apart. Luke was leaving. For all she knew, he might already be gone. She didn't know what to do about it or how to stop him.

Wearily, she let herself into her apartment, and as she did a voice railed at her. *Forget the man, Blossom.*

He doesn't want you. He doesn't love you. He doesn't want to be a part of a family. Not with you or the Maitlands.

Sniffing hard and squaring her shoulders, she put away her jacket and purse, then went into the kitchen to make coffee. As she measured grounds and water, she tried to give herself a pep talk. After all, she was a fighter. That's how she'd become Blossom the Barracuda. And though she wasn't exactly proud of all the stories and the ways she'd acquired them in the past, her success had taught her much. Mainly that a person couldn't get what they wanted in life by giving up and breaking down in tears.

She had to make Luke see reason. There had to be some way—something she could do to make him understand that he was just as worthy of love and family as the next man.

All he needed was to give himself a chance to be a part of the Maitlands. To be a brother to his siblings, a nephew to Megan. Then and only then could he ever see himself in the role of husband.

The coffeemaker gurgled its last drop. She quickly reached for a mug as thoughts began to march through her head in a procession, and they all led to the same conclusion—the answer was the Maitlands.

But what was she going to do, break her promise to Luke and tell them he was in Austin? she asked herself miserably. If she did, he might never forgive her, much less trust her.

Are you crazy, Blossom? a voice chided. *Forget about trust and forgiveness. If the man is gone none of that will matter!*

Carrying her coffee to the couch, she sat on one end and, while she sipped, stared agonizingly at the phone. If she called Megan's office at the clinic, it would be hell convincing her secretary that Blossom had legitimate news to give her boss. Getting through to R.J., who was president of the clinic, might be easier, she pondered. Or she could probably corner Anna at her wedding shop and give her the news. But Blossom quickly crossed out both those notions. Megan was the one who'd put out this search for Luke and the other missing children of Robert Maitland. She was also the head of the family. She deserved to hear the news first.

Telling herself that her love for Luke was more important than her promise to him, she went in search of her little book that held all the important private numbers she'd acquired since taking her job with *Tattle Today TV*. For once, she was going to use one in a meaningful way.

Blossom was flipping through the pages when the doorbell rang. The sound was so unexpected that she jumped and dropped the book. It skidded over the keyboard of her computer, then bounced into a wicker trash basket sitting at the corner of the desk.

"Damn! If that's Billy, I'll kill him," she muttered under her breath.

Ignoring the telephone book for the moment, she hurried to the door and glanced carefully through the peephole.

"Luke!"

She thought she'd whispered his name, but she must have actually shouted it because he heard her from the other side.

"Yes, it's me. Will you let me in before somebody spots me out here?"

Wild joy roared through her, making her hands shake as she fumbled to open the door.

The moment he stepped over the threshold, she grabbed him and held him tight against her. "Oh, Luke! I was so afraid you'd already gone!"

With her face buried against his neck and her hands clinging to his shoulders, she was impossible to resist. All night, all day, he'd thought only of her, done nothing but ached for her. Being with her again filled his heart in a way he never expected.

"I thought you wanted me to be gone," he murmured huskily. "You're supposed to be remembering what an ungrateful lout I am."

She made a sound somewhere between a laugh and a sob as she gave his shoulders a little shake. "You are! Damn your hide! But I love you, anyway."

He groaned with anguish. "Don't say that, Blossom."

She reared her head back to search his face. "Why are you here?"

A grimace tightened his features. "Not to give you false hope where you and I are concerned. So don't go getting any ideas that I'm here because I—I want to be with you."

There was something in his voice, maybe that little falter, that told her he wasn't being totally honest with himself or with her. Deciding now wasn't the time to press him, she eased casually out of his arms.

"Okay. Then why are you here? You can tell me while I fetch you a cup of coffee."

Luke watched her walk into the small kitchen area. She was wearing a little red dress that stopped a few inches above her knees. Silky stockings encased her legs and red high heels were on her feet. She looked like a delicious Christmas package just waiting for him to tear into.

"I've been packed and ready to go since early this morning," he said, taking a seat on the couch.

Her heart winced at the idea that he'd gotten so close to leaving, but just as quickly she thanked God that he'd not driven away. Carrying the coffee to him, she asked, "Why didn't you?"

He heaved out a torn breath. "I'm not sure. I kept thinking about Rafe and Laura. I haven't seen them since our parents' funeral two years ago. None of us were able to do much talking at the time."

She eased down beside him. "That's understandable. I'm sure the whole thing was tragic for all of you."

He nodded grimly. "Our father being killed wasn't a shock, but learning our mother had been with him was…hard on all of us. Then not long after the funeral I went into Witness Security and had to break off all connection with them. Other than the bits and pieces of gossip I picked up at the clinic and your show, I don't know what's been happening in their lives."

Luke had told her not to hope, but hope poured into Blossom's heart, anyway. "So you've decided you'd like to see them after all?"

He sipped his coffee and nodded. "I want to see for myself if they're really happy."

"What about R.J. and Anna? And Megan?" she asked cautiously. "Is this meeting going to include them, too?"

He shrugged. "I don't know how I feel about them. I realize they are related to me, but—I've never seen them before in my life. The only thing we have in common is Robert and that's a bad thread of connection."

She squeezed his forearm. "They won't see it that way. They'll see you as a brother who was hurt by Robert just as they were."

"I guess—" He turned a rueful look on her. "I came here because I needed to hear you say that, Blossom."

The fact that he was so uncertain, so sure that his family wouldn't love or welcome him, made Blossom's heart ache. More than anything she wanted him to be happy. Even if that meant losing him to the rich, important Maitlands.

Leaving the couch, Blossom went over to her computer desk and picked up the wastebasket.

"What are you doing?" Luke asked.

She gave him a wry glance. "Looking up Megan's telephone number."

"You keep your directory in the trash?"

She chuckled, then with a sheepish grin walked back to where he sat. "Actually, when you rang the doorbell a few minutes ago, I dropped it. I was toying with the idea of calling Megan to tell her about you."

He looked at her with wry resignation. "After I specifically asked you not to. You promised—"

Shaking her head, she hurriedly sank down beside him. "And I didn't. But I was trying to—well, I couldn't just let you leave, Luke. I had to do something!"

His lips thinned to a grim line as his gaze fell from her face to the floor. "Like I told you a few minutes ago, this whole thing about seeing my family doesn't change anything, Blossom. I am going to leave. Just not today."

She breathed deeply in hopes of easing the ache between her breasts. "Well—at least you're being honest with me. That's more than most guys are willing to do."

Luke didn't like to think of any guy telling Blossom lies or crushing her spirit. He didn't want to think of another man connected to her in the same way he felt connected. But eventually, after he went away and she began to forget, there would be someone to take his place in her heart, he thought sickly.

His gaze lifted back to her face. "Look, Blossom, you'll find someone much better suited to you than me," he told her. "Believe me."

He was the *only* man suited for her, Blossom wanted to say. Instead, she tried to focus her burning eyes on the book in her hand. "Do you want me to contact Megan for you? Or do you want to do it yourself?"

She was changing the subject completely, Luke realized. As though she'd decided to give up her quest to bring the two of them together. He should have felt immense relief that he'd finally made her see reason. Instead, he simply felt hollow.

"I'd be grateful if you'd do the calling. I don't want our first meeting to be over the telephone."

Even though he was determined to shut Blossom out of his life, she had to admire him for putting his family before himself, for risking his own life to ensure they wouldn't come to harm.

Nodding, she said, "I think Megan would appreciate that."

Over at her desk, she reached for the telephone. Yet before she could pick up the receiver, he spoke her name, causing her to pause and cast him a cautious glance.

"Don't be angry with me," he said gently. "We've been through too much together for us to end on a bad note."

She swallowed as her throat tightened. "That's just it, Luke, this shouldn't be an ending for us. It should be a new beginning."

His quiet chuckle was full of cynicism and regret. "A beginning for Luke Maitland. You're so young, Blossom. So young and naive. Men like me don't get new beginnings."

Forgetting the phone for a moment, she walked back over to the couch. "Why?" she asked, her eyes searching his face for answers. "What kind of man are you?"

He rose to his feet and her heart squeezed with pain and longing as he kissed her cheek.

"One not nearly good enough for you, Blossom." Because he couldn't resist he planted another kiss at the corner of her soft mouth. "I want you to be happy, and I'm not the man who can make you that way."

He pulled his head back from hers and Blossom looked up at him with a mixture of pain and challenge. "Just promise me one thing, Luke," she whispered.

"What's that?"

"After you see your family, you'll come by and say goodbye before you leave Austin."

What she was asking would be torture, he thought. But he couldn't deny her this one thing. As he'd told her earlier, the two of them had been through too much together for them to part on bad terms. Still, Blossom was the first woman, the only one who'd ever truly cared for him in a down-deep way. Luke had no doubts about that. Each time she touched him, looked at him, he could feel it with every fiber inside him. To walk away from that sort of caring would be a hell of a lot harder than facing a band of gunmen. But he couldn't let her know he felt that way. He had to make her believe that once he left Austin, he would never think of her again.

"All right, Blossom. I promise."

The next afternoon, Luke drove through the gated entrance of the Maitland estate, then slowly up the winding drive until he reached the stately white mansion. From all that Blossom had told him after her telephone exchange with Megan, his aunt was delighted that he'd been found and was willing to come meet the family. However, Luke wasn't quite convinced. It would be just like Blossom to gloss things over in order to make him feel better about this meeting.

At the door, he ran a hand over his newly cut hair. Having his neck exposed to the cool air felt strange, but not nearly as odd as the idea of seeing his own brothers and sisters housed in such luxury. This was the sort of people he'd guarded, not the kind he called family.

Almost immediately after he pressed the bell, the door swung back and Luke was faced with a tall, gray-haired butler, who immediately introduced himself as Harold.

"Come in, Mr. Maitland," the older man invited. "Everyone is waiting in the great room for your arrival."

He tried not to swallow as a wave of nervousness

washed over him. "With guns drawn?" he said, attempting to joke.

Harold cast him a scandalized glance. "Oh, no, Mr. Maitland. I think you'll find a celebration is waiting."

This time it was Luke's turn to be shocked, and for one split second, he considered backing out of the foyer and heading straight to his truck. *He* wasn't a reason to celebrate. He wasn't some suave 007, who made women swoon and evil criminals quake in their shoes. Blossom might think so, but everyone else knew better. Hell, right now he was homeless and unemployed. He wasn't in the same league as these Maitlands.

Thoughts of flight were still flashing through his mind as Harold opened one of two wide doors and gestured for him to enter. Luke glanced regretfully down at his jeans and boots and scarred leather jacket, then drew a deep breath and stepped into a richly furnished room.

"Luke!"

Before Luke could detect where the sound of his brother's voice was coming from, Rafe burst through the bunch of them and rushed over to where Luke remained standing just inside the door.

Smiling broadly, Rafe gripped Luke's hand and pumped it heartily. "We've all been waiting a long time for this, big brother. I think all of us were about to believe you couldn't be found."

Still uncertain, Luke studied the brother he'd not seen in two years. On first glance, Rafe appeared to be the same as he remembered. A tall, strong cowboy with the same brown hair and green eyes. But this Rafe exuded a happy confidence he'd never seen before.

"Were you really hunting for me?" Luke asked.

Laughing, Rafe turned to the crowd behind him. "Hey, everyone, Luke wants to know if we've really been trying to find him."

Groans and happy laughs of disbelief filled the room. Dismayed by it all, Luke continued to focus on his brother for answers. "I don't understand, Rafe—"

"Believe me, Luke, I know what you're going through right now. When I got word that Aunt Megan wanted me to come here and meet with the family— well, let's just say I'm glad I didn't let memories of Dad keep me from doing it."

"But—"

"Luke, aren't you going to give me a hug?"

At the sound of his sister Laura's voice, he turned and felt his heart melt as he saw her outstretched arms.

Stepping forward, he enveloped her in a tight embrace. "Hello, Laura," he murmured close to her ear.

Once she finally released him, Laura eased back and studied him with happy, tear-filled eyes. "What a sight you are!" she cried. "That black hair is really something. I thought Elvis had stepped into the room."

With a self-conscious grin he rubbed at the sideburns he'd not yet shaved off. "You wished."

Laughing tearfully, she tugged on his arm. "You're the celebrity I wanted to see."

Luke touched a finger to her pretty cheek. The last time he'd seen her, she'd been shattered by their mother's death. It filled his heart with joy to see that like Rafe, Laura, too, looked happy, even contented. "Yeah," he murmured, "it's been too long."

"Not since…the funeral," Laura replied.

He suddenly felt his younger brother's hand on his shoulder and the warm weight brought back memories of long ago when the four of them had huddled together and waited for the yells of their father to quiet into drunken snores. Clinging to one another had been a way for them to survive back then. Now it was still just as good to know he wasn't alone. At least for this day in his life.

"Yeah, we're all together," Rafe said happily, then with grim regret added, "except for Janelle. I guess you've heard about her and all the damage she caused the family?"

Luke nodded somberly. "Janelle was always different from the three of us. I guess none of us understood just how different she really was. The thing that amazes me is that Megan and her family would want any of us around after all the misery Janelle inflicted on them."

"Megan is a generous, loving woman, Luke," Laura said. "She's made us a part of the family—just as if we were her own children."

"That's true," Rafe agreed, then made a motion with his head toward the back of the room where the rest of the Maitlands stood waiting. "Come on, Luke. It's time you met her, and your new brother and sister."

"And your new nieces," Laura added proudly as she looped her arm through his. "You do know that I'm a mother now and Rafe will soon be a father? His wife, Greer, has just learned that she's expecting."

Luke laughed with disbelief. "I heard it through the clinic grapevine, but I wasn't sure I could believe it. My little brother and sister being a mommy and daddy,'' he said wryly. ''I guess I didn't realize the two of you were that grown up.''

Rafe glanced at him with wishful speculation. ''We were hoping you'd have a family by now.''

Luke laughed again, however this time the sound was hollow. ''Not in my line of work, brother. I'm a living target—not a good candidate for a husband or father.''

Rafe and Laura exchanged regretful glances. Between them, Luke tried to stop thinking of Blossom.

For the next thirty minutes or more, Luke met his family. The first to greet him warmly were his new in-laws, Rafe's wife, Greer, and Laura's husband, Mick, and their new daughter. Then there were his half siblings R.J. and Anna. Also there to meet him were the rest of Megan's children: Mitchell, Jake, Abby, Ellie, Beth and Connor, who, unlike the other children, had not been fathered by William Maitland but rather by Clyde Mitchum during a teenage love affair with Megan.

It was Connor who had been the target of Janelle and Petey's evil plans. The two of them had kidnapped his baby son and also nearly killed his wife Lacy. Janelle had delivered such a severe blow to her head, it had taken months for the young woman to regain her memory.

Luke was amazed to see the couple and their child, Chase, here at this little homecoming for him. But then he still couldn't quite believe that these Maitlands wanted anything to do with Robert and Veronica's children. Yet they were all quickly proving him wrong with their handshakes and smiles and affectionate slaps on the shoulder.

As more people were introduced to him, he tried

to keep their names and faces in order, but after a while there were too many for him to deal with. However, there was one name and face that Luke had no trouble remembering. His aunt Megan with her white hair and tall, regal appearance stood out like a polished diamond. Luke was not only impressed by her appearance; he was immediately drawn to the older woman's warmth and sincerity. In no time at all, she'd put him at ease, insisted he call her Megan and generally made him feel as though he belonged among this group of people. Even if only for today.

A long time later, after coffee and cake had been served, Megan took Luke into her private office where she showed him a family picture album of past ancestors and explained how the Maitland dynasty had come to be. By the time she was finished, Luke had a much better understanding of his roots and why his aunt had felt that it was so important to locate Robert's missing offspring. Family was everything to the woman, even family members like him who were not so perfect.

"I'm really surprised that Miss Woodward didn't come with you today," Megan told him as she placed the photo album safely back in her desk. "I did invite her."

From the first moment he'd arrived at the mansion, Luke had tried to focus solely on his relatives and push Blossom from his mind. But so far he was lucky if he could go ten seconds without thinking about the blond, blue-eyed beauty. He would have felt more comfortable if she'd been here with him today. She was like his arm or leg. She was a part of him, and without her he felt something was missing. But he'd stopped himself from inviting her to accompany him.

He didn't want to give her any false impression of the two of them as a couple. And, too, he'd not wanted to offend the Maitlands with her presence.

"I—uh, wasn't aware that you'd invited her," Luke admitted to Megan. "She didn't mention it to me."

Megan's brows drew together in a faint frown. "I was looking forward to thanking her. I have a feeling she was responsible for you being here today."

Luke's gaze dropped away from his aunt's. "She was...somewhat responsible. I was going to leave town. But she made me see I wouldn't be doing any of you right if I simply left without a word."

"She's a smart woman."

Surprised, Luke looked at Megan. "While I was working at the clinic, I got the notion that this family didn't like her. She has reported some things I'm sure you'd rather not have had aired to the public."

Sighing, Megan reached for a cup and saucer sitting at one corner of her desk. When she settled her gaze directly on Luke, a strong awareness flashed through him, and he suddenly understood that this woman would always be willing to stand in for the mother he'd lost.

"We've had our ups and downs with Chelsea Markum and Blossom," Megan admitted. "But I'm not narrow-minded, Luke. I realize the woman is only trying to do a job. And whether I like that job or not is beside the point. I have to give her points for doing it well."

Megan came back around the desk and he waited for her to take a seat in a nearby armchair, before he made a reply.

"She's not really the brash reporter you see on television, Megan. Beneath all that, she's a different person.''

An understanding smile touched the older woman's face. ''So you got to know her a little during this whole incident.''

Luke nodded as warm, tender memories of Blossom poured through him. He'd never met a woman who could fight so tough or love so much. She was one of a kind. She was in his heart and he didn't know how or if he could ever get her out.

''She's never had things easy. Her childhood wasn't as bad as the one my siblings and I went through. But it was enough to scar her. She's driven to succeed—I think because as a child she never received the love or security she needed. Her parents were very poor providers and I guess she's going a bit overboard trying not to be like them.''

''Sounds like you've gotten close to her.''

His throat was suddenly too thick to speak so he merely nodded.

''This will probably make me sound like a nosy old woman, but do you plan to build a relationship with her?''

Luke drew in a deep breath, then let it out slowly, but the dull ache around his heart refused to go away.

''No. I'm—leaving Austin. Tomorrow.''

Her brows arched upward. ''Because of Blossom or for other reasons?''

Luke started to lie and state other reasons for his need to leave town. But he didn't want this woman getting the notion that he was really leaving to avoid living around this big Maitland family.

''Because of Blossom,'' he answered truthfully.

"And why is that? I've been getting the impression you care for her a great deal."

"I do. I love her." There. He'd said it, damn it. Not only to himself, but also to his aunt.

Megan solemnly shook her head. "Then I don't understand, Luke. Love isn't something you can turn your back on and expect to find it elsewhere. I think Rafe and Laura would understand that."

At the mention of his brother and sister, he smiled wanly. "I'm glad they're married now and are both so happy. They deserve it."

"And you don't?"

He stared at her. "You can't put me on the same shelf as Rafe and Laura."

"Why not?"

His hand lifted from the arm of the chair, then fell helplessly back down. "Because I'm different. I'm older. I've seen things and was forced to do things that would shock you."

She smiled at him. "So have I."

He groaned. "Not like me."

Another knowing smile crossed her face. "You'd be surprised, Luke."

He rose from his chair and walked over to a window that looked out over a back garden. Many of the plants had grown dormant during the cooler fall weather, but the grass was still green and a few roses continued to bloom along a rock wall. The beauty of the flowers reminded Luke even more of Blossom.

"She deserves more than me and what I can give her."

Megan left her chair and walked over to where he stood. When she placed her hand on his shoulder, he turned and looked at her with surprise. He'd expected some motherly advice from this woman, but not a comforting hand to go with it.

"I've been known to be wrong about people before, Luke. God knows my trusting Janelle and Petey was downright foolish. And now Clyde has come along and, well, nearly made a fool of me again. If he hadn't had a change of heart and confessed that he was the one making all that mischief at the clinic—well…"

Earlier this afternoon his brother Rafe, had told him about Clyde's confession and his misguided intention to get money from Megan. The news of the older man's misbehavior had surprised Luke along with the fact that Megan had already forgiven Clyde.

"You might have ruined a good thing with Hugh Blake," he finished for her.

She laughed softly, and to Luke's surprise there was a tinge of pink on her cheeks. "I wasn't aware that you knew about Hugh. He's the attorney for Maitland Maternity."

"Yes, Blossom told me. She seems to think that you should be looking in his direction."

She blushed again, then patted his shoulder. "Blossom knows a good man when she sees one. And so do I. I've made a few slip-ups on judging character, but not where you're concerned. You saved Blossom's life and you put your own in danger in order to protect your family. You're a good man, Luke."

Tormented, he closed his eyes to the beauty of the garden and the vision of Blossom's lovely face. Seeing his brother and sister today with their spouses and children had made him hunger for the same. He wanted to be needed and included in a family circle of his own, but that didn't necessarily mean he would know how to hold up his end of a marriage bargain.

"I don't know anything about being a husband, Megan. Or even a long-term companion. And God help me if I ever became a father—"

"You would try your best," Megan interrupted. "That's where you're different from Robert. He was a selfish man. He didn't care enough to try to be a father. You would. And that's all any of us can do."

Luke hoped she was right, because he was slowly beginning to see that he needed this Maitland family. And he needed Blossom even more.

Blossom tossed down the pen and rubbed her weary eyes. For the past three hours she'd been working nonstop on a story she'd been trying to put together for several months now. During her investigations for *Tattle Today,* she'd run across many children who'd been affected by negligent parents, some of them tragically so. Over the months she'd saved notes and bits of information with plans to somehow thread them all together into one piece that might be good enough to capture someone's attention.

She glanced down at the yellow legal notepad with its pages of handwritten notes. The story wouldn't be fodder for *Tattle Today.* In fact, Billy would probably laugh if he knew of her project. But Billy would never see it, she promised herself. Unless she was lucky enough to get one of the major Texas newspapers to publish it and then she'd have the pleasure of shoving it under his nose.

But right now that was a dream. And before she could do anything with the story, she had to finish it.

Sighing, she rose from her seat and walked over to

the one window in her apartment that looked out over the street. In the pool of light from the street lamp, she could see that a light rain had started to fall. The cool, dreary weather was a perfect match for her mood, she thought sadly.

Luke's meeting with the Maitlands had been hours ago, and since she'd neither seen nor heard from him, she could only conclude that he'd broken his promise and left Austin without saying goodbye to her.

Once or twice this evening she'd considered driving by his house just to see if his truck was there or if the place was already deserted. In the end, she'd chosen to stay put in her apartment and face the fact that the old adage about the horse was true. Leading him to water didn't necessarily mean he would drink. She'd tried to lead Luke in her direction, but he'd decided to go the opposite way. There was nothing more she could do about it, except try to forget him.

With tears burning her eyes, she turned away from the window and headed back to her desk. Maybe if she tried again, she could get her mind to focus.

More than thirty minutes and ten words later, the sound of the doorbell cut into her anguished thoughts.

Certain this time that it was Billy coming to harass her about getting back to work, she stalked to the door and jerked it open without even looking through the peephole.

The moment she spotted Luke standing on the small square of concrete porch, her mouth fell open. "Luke! I thought—you aren't gone yet!"

"No," he said. "I've just now got away from the Maitland mansion."

All she could do was stare at him. His hair was

short, his face was shaved. Cowboy boots were on his feet and a lopsided smile was on his face.

"May I come in?"

His question galvanized her into action. Quickly she stepped out of the door and motioned for him to enter. He brushed past her and entered into the room. A faint scent of rain and musk trailed after him.

Blossom shut the door, then turned to face him with a sense of foreboding. "So I suppose you're on your way out of the city," she said in a voice so strained she could hardly hear it herself.

He stepped toward her, and as he did one hand emerged from his back. It was carrying a pink rose. Not a cultivated hothouse rose that could be purchased at any number of stores, but one grown in a real garden.

"Actually, I'm not."

"You're going tomorrow?"

He stepped closer and Blossom's heart kicked into a wild tap dance against her breast.

"That depends on you."

Her eyes flew wide. "Me?"

His smile was suddenly sheepish. "Yes, you."

He thrust the rose at her. Blossom accepted it, her expression both wondrous and bemused. "What is this for?"

"It's from a garden at the Maitland mansion. It reminded me of you. Not perfect, but very beautiful and precious just the same."

A sob caught in her throat and it was long moments before she could speak. "Don't say such things, Luke, if you're planning on walking out the door. I can't—I'm not strong enough for that."

"And I'm not strong enough to say goodbye."

Her eyes met his, and then with a cry of anguish and hope, she flung her arms around him and buried her face against his neck. "Do you mean that, Luke? Really mean it?" she murmured.

"I wouldn't be here if I didn't, Blossom. I may not deserve you, but I have to have you in my life. Maybe that's hard for you to believe, but——"

She eased her head back far enough to allow her gaze to search his face. "What made you change your mind? Last night you were so adamant about leaving, about me finding someone else."

"I must have been out of my mind to think I could have let another man even look at you," he growled.

Thrilled by the possessive tone of his voice, she snuggled the rest of her body close to his. "You should have known there wasn't any danger of that happening. You've ruined me, Luke Maitland. I'm a one-man woman and you're that man."

He groaned with relief. "I was so afraid that, after all I'd said last night, I'd ruined everything between us."

She shook her head. "I kept trying to tell myself you didn't mean half of it. I kept praying the meeting with your family would somehow make you see that you needed me."

"Oh, Blossom, my brother and sister are so happy. Megan and R.J. and Anna, they were all so—I couldn't believe the reception they gave me. Everyone was there—just like I was *somebody*. Somebody they wanted in the family."

Giving his shoulders an affectionate shake, she said, "You shouldn't have thought they would feel any other way."

"I ended up staying for hours. And during that time Megan and I had a discussion about you."

Blossom was shocked. "I guess she'll never forgive me for some of the stories I reported on *Tattle Today*. But maybe I can convince her I wasn't doing it as a personal vendetta."

Luke shook his head. "She doesn't hate you, Blossom. I don't think it's in Megan to hate anyone. In fact, I think she admires you for doing your job so well. But your job wasn't the crux of our discussion. It was about me and you."

She stared at him. "You mean—you told her how I feel about you?"

He smiled. "No. I told her how *I* feel about you. And she made me realize I couldn't walk away from what we could have together. I love you too much. I have to stay here in Austin and try to make you happy."

Showering sparks of joy exploded inside her. "You won't have to, my darling. You've already made me very happy."

She brought her lips up to his and he took them in a deep, promising kiss that spoke not only of the love he felt for her at this moment, but for all the years to come.

Once he lifted his head, contentment purred in her throat. "Now are you ready to make love to me?"

His hands tightened on her waist as he scattered tempting kisses across her upturned face. "Blossom, I've wanted to make love to you since the moment I met you. But good things come to those who wait. And you've been waiting a long time for the right man. Our wedding night won't be that far away."

Groaning with good-natured acceptance, she pulled out of his arms and headed to the kitchen.

"If that's the case, I'd better put this rose in some water before you scorch both of us."

A week later Megan's long-planned family reunion finally became true. In honor of the special occasion and the upcoming holidays, the Maitland mansion had been turned into a Christmas fairyland with decorations filling every nook and corner. In each room a trimmed tree glowed with hundreds of bubbling lights. Poinsettias, blooming Christmas cacti and lighted candles graced tables and fireplace mantels.

Since the great room was the gathering spot for the event, it had been decorated even more lavishly. Several towering Christmas trees trimmed in red and gold were clustered along one whole wall to create an extravagant grove of evergreen. The scent of pine and spruce filled the air and mingled with the spicy food laid out on long tables.

In one corner, a string quartet played everything from "Silent Night" to "Rockin' Around the Christmas Tree" while couples danced on an open area of hardwood floor. Wine and champagne flowed, along with spirited eggnog and fruit punch. Laughter could be heard from one side of the giant room to the other as the entire Maitland family and their spouses enjoyed the feasting and music and the wonderful fact that all of them were finally together.

Out on the dance floor, in the tight circle of Luke's arm, Blossom was a picture of beautiful bliss in a royal-blue velvet gown, her long blond hair twisted into a cluster of golden curls atop her head. On her hand was a diamond-and-emerald engagement ring that Luke had given her only hours before. Now, as her hand lay on his shoulder and he whirled her to the music, the brilliant stones winked back at her.

"I think you'd better keep pinching me, darling," she whispered in his ear. "I'm beginning to feel like a princess."

Laughing, he discreetly gave her bottom a naughty caress. "Honey, I'm not a prince."

"You are to me," she whispered, then, because the temptation was too great, she kissed his smoothly shaven cheek.

"I'm glad you're enjoying tonight. You were so nervous before we got here."

"That's because I didn't know how your family was going to take the news that we were going to be married on New Year's Eve. I'm certain some of them considered me the *enemy*."

"That was before the shooting," Luke pointed out. "Now they see you as a heroine for saving me from the Liberators."

Blossom laughed at the idea of herself in such a lofty role. It was quite a switch from Blossom the Barracuda. But thankfully the Maitlands were beginning to understand that her job at *Tattle Today TV* was only a stepping-stone and that now she wanted to break into serious journalism and focus on children's issues.

Teasingly, she said, "At the time, I vaguely remember you saying you hadn't needed my help and that you could have handled everything all by yourself."

He gave her pert little bottom another loving pat. "That was only male arrogance talking. I'm going to always need your help, honey. Always."

"That's good to hear. But I'm more than certain you can handle your new job without your wife's meddling."

Since his homecoming a week ago, Megan and the rest of the family had asked him to take over the role of head of security for Maitland Maternity. Luke hadn't needed long to make up his mind to accept the position. The idea of working for family at a much less dangerous job was exactly what he wanted. As soon as he and Blossom returned from their honeymoon, he planned to assume the full duties of the post. In the meantime, he was already busy making changes for the better in the old security system.

"I'm flattered they think I can be trusted with the job. Especially since the clinic has had some serious problems with security this past year."

"That's why they want an expert like you to make sure everything and everyone is kept safe," Blossom told him, then glanced across the floor to where Megan was dancing with Hugh Blake. "I'm so glad your aunt can finally put all that behind her and look toward the future. She and Hugh are going to be happy together."

"How can you be so sure?" Luke asked.

Blossom gave him a look that said she couldn't believe he had to ask. "Because I can see the sparks between them."

Luke chuckled. "Are you seeing that as a reporter or a woman?"

Without a word, Blossom led him off the dance floor and through a set of tall French doors that opened onto the garden. Stopping beside one of the rose-covered walls, she slipped her arms around his neck.

"Now for your answer," she murmured. "I'm seeing those sparks as a woman and I've decided it's time we create some of our own."

He groaned with sweet pleasure as her lips pressed against his. "I can see it's going to be hell trying to control you until our wedding night."

"You're not going to tie me to a chair again, are you?"

His sexy laugh fanned her cheeks. "Wouldn't you like to know."

* * * * *

Celebrate the season with

Midnight Clear

**A holiday anthology featuring
a classic Christmas story from
New York Times bestselling author**

Debbie Macomber

**Plus a brand-new *Morgan's Mercenaries* story
from *USA Today* bestselling author**

Lindsay McKenna

**And a brand-new *Twins on the Doorstep* story
from national bestselling author**

Stella Bagwell

Available at your favorite retail outlets in November 2001!

Silhouette®

Where love comes alive™

Visit Silhouette at www.eHarlequin.com   PSMC

CALL THE ONES YOU LOVE OVER THE HOLIDAYS!

Save $25 off future book purchases when you buy any four Harlequin® or Silhouette® books in October, November and December 2001,

PLUS

receive a phone card good for 15 minutes of long-distance calls to anyone you want in North America!

WHAT AN INCREDIBLE DEAL!

Just fill out this form and attach 4 proofs of purchase (cash register receipts) from October, November and December 2001 books, and Harlequin Books will send you a coupon booklet worth a total savings of $25 off future purchases of Harlequin® and Silhouette® books, AND a 15-minute phone card to call the ones you love, anywhere in North America.

Please send this form, along with your cash register receipts as proofs of purchase, to:
In the USA: Harlequin Books, P.O. Box 9057, Buffalo, NY 14269-9057
In Canada: Harlequin Books, P.O. Box 622, Fort Erie, Ontario L2A 5X3
Cash register receipts must be dated no later than December 31, 2001.
Limit of 1 coupon booklet and phone card per household.
Please allow 4-6 weeks for delivery.

I accept your offer! Please send me my coupon booklet and a 15-minute phone card:

Name: _____

Address: _____ City: _____

State/Prov.: _____ Zip/Postal Code: _____

Account Number (if available): _____

---

097 KJB DAGL
PHQ4012

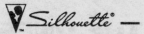